THE LADY OF THE GARTER

LADIES OF LORE BOOK I

MARISA DILLON

CROWN & CASTLE
PUBLISHING

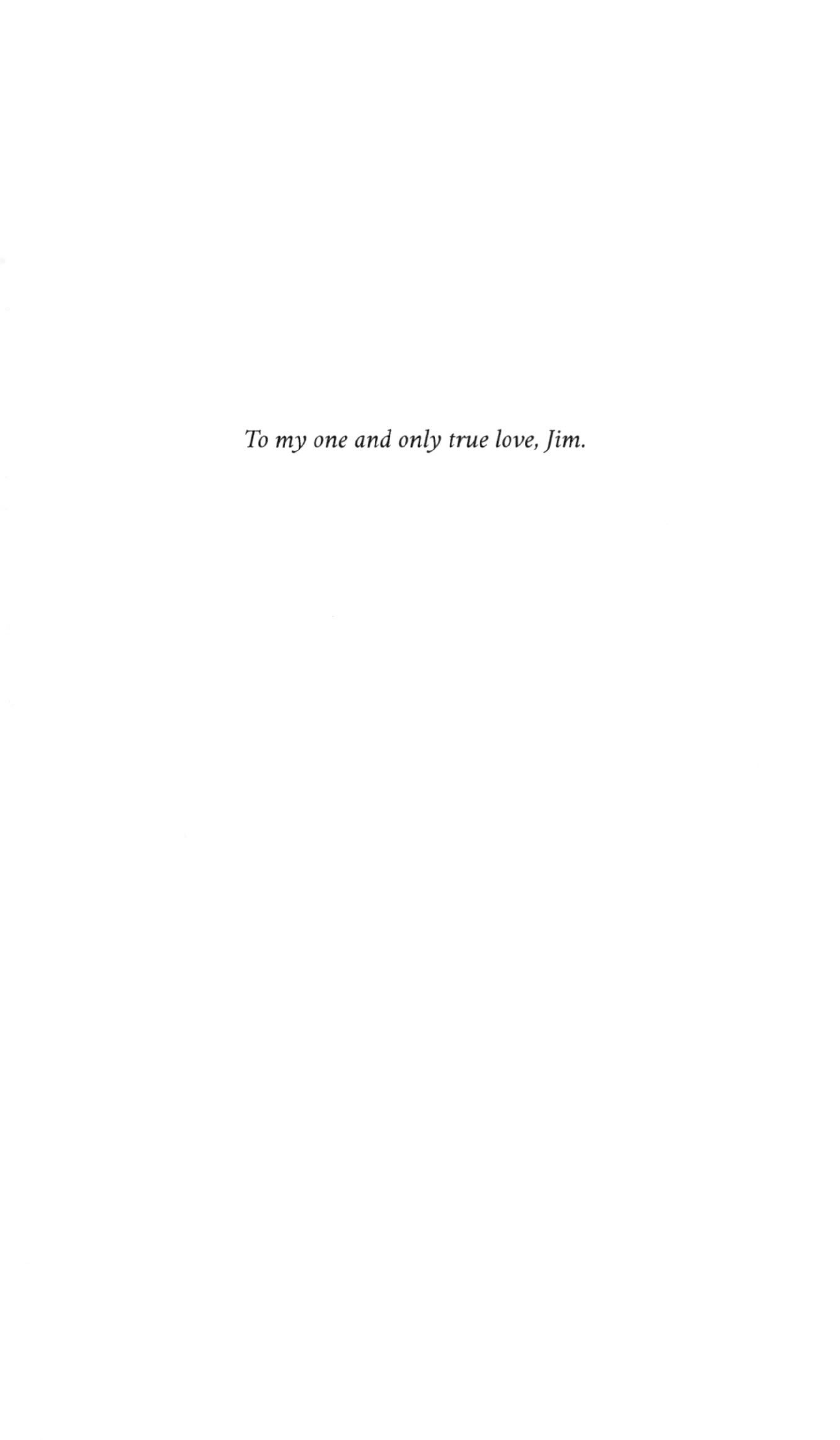

To my one and only true love, Jim.

ACKNOWLEDGMENTS

The author would like to thank:

The professionals: author Terri Valentine, who mentored me to publication; Violetta Rand, my editor, whose direction and vision I trusted; Karin Shah, who lighted the path to publication; and industry professional, Debby Gilbert, who discovered me.

My family: son Zach, who always asked, "Mom, how's the book coming?" He never doubted my weekend musings would become a book; son Jamie, who gave me his creative support in so many ways; my parents Alf and Celia Hansen, who took me all over the world as a young girl, influencing my storytelling today; my brother, Eric, writer and author; my supportive sister, Carina; my Aunt Linda, who encouraged me to start writing in her Cape Cod retreat years ago and told me I could do this; and my husband, Jim, my modern-day knight.

My friends: so many to thank, but particularly Robin Michaels, who never doubted; Melissa Johnson, who helped me in more ways than I can count; and my advisor, Jeff Bruce, whose guidance was essential.

Without their support, this book would not have been written.

CHAPTER 1

arwick Castle, Warwickshire 1486

The new King of England had taken the throne only yesterday, but not all were loyal to Henry. That wasn't what troubled Lady Elena as she raised her hood and quickened her pace. She skirted around two squires dragging a dead knight by his boots from the tournament field.

When she reached the weapons pavilion at the end of the castle's lower bailey, she pulled the flap open and went inside. Thankfully, the thick cloth filtered out some of the noise coming from the jousting arena, the cheers and clashing metal.

It took a while for her eyes to adjust to the dim. Already desperate to find her brother, Elena searched the enclosure. Lances, longswords, buckler shields, and battle-axes lined the walls. She approached the center of the space unsure of what made her feel so uncomfortable. Lack of sleep? A general discomfort for what she was expected to do today? *That's* what disturbed her—the lie she was about to live, the secret she was expected to keep.

An imposing figure turned abruptly, then came toward her.

She screamed.

"Elena, it's all right," a familiar voice called.

She sighed with relief, glad to have found her brother, but her trepidation quickly turned to anger.

"William," she said, jerking off her winter cloak. "I cannot honor our promise."

He waved an impatient hand. "Sir James is next on the field. There's no one else to squire. He needs three able bodies to assist him. Jacob, me, *and you*. There's no time to discuss your doubts and hesitation. You *will* do this."

So this was the way of it? Her feelings were unimportant? "I—I cannot go through with it." She wanted a chance to explain, but didn't know where to begin. If she waited too long, he'd choose for her. It had been a foolish idea from the start.

"Elena, you *will* honor our arrangement. You made a vow to God. I was there to witness it, remember?" He was losing patience. He walked to the rear of the tent, ignoring her, then began rooting through the lances in the corner.

She fisted her hands and found the courage to voice her opinion. Although intimidating, she wasn't really afraid of her brother. Besides, oath breaking bothered her more than his hulking figure.

"Hear me, Brother, tis all *your* doing. I only wished for a chance to see James again. But not this way." She eyed the ugly boy's clothing she was wearing with disgust.

William still paid her no attention, so she grabbed his arm, but he wrenched free, studying her appearance with a smirk.

She wore a loose-fitting linen tunic that hid her breasts. Baggy, tanned leather knickers concealed the rest of her figure, completing the masculine disguise.

He nodded with approval. "Tis time, Elena. You are ready. Admit it. Once I confirmed Sir James's entry for the tournament, you jumped at the chance to be here," he accused her. "You concocted this scheme."

"Me?" she said, glowering. "No, I wanted training, not this." Elena dug into her pocket, then presented a handful of her dark auburn locks.

He scowled. "That's only further proof of your guilt. You can't blame me. I didn't hold you down to shear you like a lamb. You volunteered. We're equally guilty. Admit it, and quit complaining."

Tears stung her eyes. She threw the hair to the ground.

He shook his head, his deep brown eyes as unreadable as always. Then he reached into his nearby satchel and produced a gray-blue wool cap, which he immediately threw at her. "Here, you'll need this."

She glared at him while she tucked her shoulder-length hair under the hat.

"No more delays. You are now squire to Sir James. I gave my word. Take hold of this." He tilted a lance toward her.

Elena sighed, grabbing it the way she wanted to hold on to his throat. She was getting nowhere with him. "Where you go, I suppose I must follow," she grumbled. No one challenged her brother. He was large and tall like their father, with curly, chestnut brown hair, worn in a tail at the nape of his neck. Although bearded, he still possessed a youthful face.

Now he provoked her with a tug of the weapon and a laugh, dragging her outside. She followed him silently through the large crowd.

The tournament had drawn visitors from most every shire in England. The new king was celebrating his marriage and his assent to the throne with a lavish commemoration.

Elena had to trot to keep up, as her brother wove through the throng. Peasants, clergy, knights, and nobles alike were on their way to the tournament stands and didn't care about who or what they were today—only the chance to watch the fights. And Elena dared not protest. A woman dressed as a lad would draw unwanted attention, and likely get her into trouble.

Chivalry remained much disputed in the realm, and today's *pas d'armes* was an attempt by the king to settle the debate. The War of the Roses had raged on for more than thirty years between the houses of York and Lancaster. Loyalties had been tested, ambitions questioned. Heirs remained unconfirmed. With Henry's victory over Richard the III at the battle of Bosworth Field, under the banner of the Red Dragon, he'd assumed the crown. Demanded it.

Instead of warring, today the contestants would fight for the pleasure of the people.

So was the intent.

It didn't take long to reach the field and the list area roped off for the competition. They headed toward the closest palisade fence that separated the knights from the onlookers. Without warning, William stopped at the first list, knocking Elena on her rump.

Laughter erupted from the crowd. Her cheeks burned as she stood and gave her brother a nasty look. She wanted to disappear from sight. Brushing the dirt off her arse, she tried to stay focused on her purpose, *finding James.*

She couldn't see much of anything above the multitude that had gathered. Regardless, her heart quickened as she pushed through the narrow path between the stands and tilt-yard. She swore under her breath as she climbed the palisade fence, trying to spot James.

A group of boys, full of more than mischief, nearly knocked her off her perch before she found her knight on the field.

Her breath caught when she eyed the too familiar golden

mane of hair. It whipped wildly in the wind. Sitting atop his warhorse in full armor, he did not disappoint. He was everything she'd imagined and remembered. He radiated courage, strength, nobility, and pride. She pitied his opponent.

Close enough to catch his attention with a shout, the temptation passed quickly. Instead, she would admire his handsome features. With a square jaw, a narrow straight nose, and a wicked smile, he represented everything she'd always been attracted to in a man. He was exquisitely made. She'd seen tapestries of the Greek Gods and even they could not compare.

Oh yes, and those steel-blue eyes, they were the same color of the three lions emblazoned on his shield. His black destrier wore matching marks on its ornamented trapper and pawed the ground impatiently, as ready for action as his esteemed rider.

William startled her when he grabbed her by the waist and attempted to pull her off the fence. She resisted, slapping at his hands. No, she didn't want to take her eyes off her knight. Not yet. Never. She'd waited too long for this moment.

"You there, Squire," a noble shouted to William above the fray, "who are the knights that take up their arms on the tournament field?"

William let go.

"God's teeth, didn't you check the lists?" William answered. "Tis Sir James and Sir Hugh, both Garter knight champions. With King Henry in attendance, will make for a fine competition."

"No. I just arrived at Warwick Castle from the north," the man explained. "I ask not about these knights now," he said, pointing toward the jousting area. "Who was the champion just leaving the field? The victor with the bloodied lance?"

"Sir Nicholas, the king's cousin," William answered, then

leaned against the railing behind him. "What is the importance?"

"The man's brutal style of fighting. I thought this tourney was in honor of the king's marriage. Why the excessive violence?"

Elena could have answered. Her father had warned her about Sir Nicholas Luttrell. Although relatively unknown in Warwickshire, his sordid family history wasn't. The man lived beyond the law. And now that he was part of the new House of Tudor, uniting the Yorkists and Lancastrians, he made his own decrees. Yet, this newly appointed Earl of Dunster, still lived in obscurity. No one outside the royal family had seen him in years, until today. And even then, he'd been helmeted while on the field.

A trumpet blast interrupted Elena's thoughts. It also silenced the crowd. Everyone watched as the next competitors prepared to enter the field.

Elena eyed her brother's friend, Jacob, the third squire who was assigned to James. He would manage the armor and was ready with the lances. She wouldn't be needed until later, affording her time to watch the match from the sidelines.

She laughed nervously as James struggled to tame his wind-blown mane before covering it with his helmet. Now fully dressed, he took the lance from Jacob. With all the ceremonial decorum completed, the knights' restless mounts were released.

Elena squeezed her eyes shut, afraid of what was to come. But the sounds of snapping lances and snorting warhorses forced them open again. Damn her curiosity.

The knights rounded their barriers, retrieving fresh weapons after dropping the broken ones. By the time their horses reached the center of the field again, the lances smashed together. Wood splintered in all directions, even hitting some spectators low in the stands.

James's horse reared up.

Then both dropped their lances.

Sir Hugh waved his arms wildly, as if he was trying to grab an imaginary rope to steady himself. He let his shield fall.

The crowd cheered as the knights struggled to stay seated.

Unfortunately, James hit the ground first, bucked violently from the saddle. Elena gasped. Her knight was motionless and silent. Was he dead? She prayed not. Then her gaze slid to Sir Hugh, whose efforts to stay mounted were in vain. He too tumbled off his horse.

For a moment, neither moved.

"El—Edward, to the champion's tent," William shouted. "You are the squire assigned to remove the armor. We need you at the ready." He hurried out to the main field.

Ignoring her brother's command, she climbed through the tilt ropes that separated the combatants' lanes instead. She wanted to get closer to James, needed to see he was still alive.

"Oh, Lord . . ." She rushed forward. "He must live." She had just found him again. She held her breath as William lifted James up to a sitting position. Two other boys offered their help.

To her surprise, Sir Hugh moved on his own, moaning in pain. His squires managed to set him on his feet, and he waved at the mesmerized crowd.

"Take the helmet off first, Squire," a man shouted to William.

To Elena's relief, a field surgeon joined her brother. Determined to help too, she snapped into action.

"William," she pleaded at his side, "I'm here."

"Edward, was my command not clear?" He glared at her, his jaw twitching. "Go."

She jumped back as if bitten. "To the tent? B-but." She couldn't think clearly. There was no use arguing now.

Her gaze dropped to James's limp body. It took every ounce of control she had to keep from getting on her knees to comfort him. Then, realizing she shouldn't be there, she walked away. This wasn't what she had expected. She'd watched her four brothers in competitions before. Yet, after all these years, seeing James beaten down struck a deep fear in her.

She entered the pavilion and waited impatiently for her brother to arrive. How in God's name had William convinced her that any of this was right? She had agreed to the scheme with the intent of meeting James again. Five years had passed since he'd left her to become a knight. Promises he'd made to her were *never* kept and she wanted to know why. Regardless, she must keep a clear mind if she was going to achieve her goal.

A commotion erupted outside. She looked at the entrance just as someone burst through.

"Squire, get this blasted armor off."

James? She couldn't move. This was the first time he'd spoken to her, the first time she'd been so close to him since she was a young girl. Her heart raced as she stared at him, speechless.

"Squire," he shouted again.

He's alive. Praised be the saints.

His rage-filled, blue gaze locked on her. Where was William?

"My lord," she said with as much confidence as she could muster. She lowered her chin, shielding her face with the brim of her cap. "I shall make quick work of the armor. Let me start with the leg braces."

"I give the commands. My grand guarde, it must be removed first."

James sat down hard on a long wooden worktable. It shook under his weight, but it was the only suitable surface available in the tent.

She grabbed a stool so she could reach the shield bolted to his breastplate. She had seen this style of armor before, even worked on fastenings in her father's workshop. Praise the Virgin Mary, at least she knew her way around a suit of armor.

She was quick about it, and soon had the upper plate off. Before she realized it though, she was eye level with his muscular chest. Too close. Completely distracted, she inched away, tumbling off the stool, landing in a heap at his feet.

Embarrassed, heat rose in her cheeks, but she looked up anyway. He towered over her. The intense gaze she met unnerved her. This was the man she'd loved. And if she allowed her emotions to override her control, he'd recognize her. She quickly looked away.

In truth, now that they were together again, all she wanted to do was rush into his arms, to feel his powerful caresses. A kiss? Oh, yes, she wanted one. But not dressed as a boy. No, she'd better act like one to protect her true identity. She shook her head.

James grunted. "Come lad, remove the leg braces."

She couldn't move.

"Squire," he rumbled. "Did you lose your mind along with your balance? The leg braces, *now*." He'd obviously run out of patience.

Minutes later, after she'd completed his command, all he wore was linen breeches. She had to turned her back to him and hide her reaction.

"Your first time?"

"My lord?" she asked. She must learn to conceal her embarrassment.

"Your first tournament? Surely, a village nurse maid could have been more efficient," he snapped. "You are dismissed."

Dismissed? She hadn't expected that. A mere moment in his presence hadn't satisfied her growing need to see him, hear him, touch him.

Not trusting herself with him any longer, she scrambled outside. The cool breeze felt good on her hot face. Damn her feelings. The disguise she wore couldn't cover up her feminine heart.

The crowd had thinned. She walked slowly down the row of temporary structures that dotted the large field. Where was her incorrigible brother? *Men.* What had she expected from this reunion? Tears of joy? A marriage proposal? She'd nearly failed at her duties. A mixture of thoughts raced through her mind.

Then she found herself completely distracted by an odd scent coming from a pavilion close to the castle. She stopped and sniffed the air. Musk and jasmine? No flag identified the occupant. What knight used incense? Unable to resist the urge to find out, Elena peeked inside. No tourney tent she'd ever seen looked or smelled this pleasant. She stepped inside.

"I can keep your secrets, *Señorita,* but can you guard the ones I give you?"

Elena stepped back in surprise.

"Come, *buena Señorita,* come in, do not be shy. Take a seat, *si,* take a seat," a soft voice invited.

Is she hiding?

Elena scanned the enclosure, hoping to spot the woman who invited her in. She was instantly drawn to an area with brightly colored pillows on the floor. They formed a circle around a low table situated in the center of the tent. With some trepidation, she knelt on the purple and gold cushion closest to her.

"Looks can be deceiving. One may appear as a woman one day, a boy the next. What game do you play?"

Only William and her cousin, Isabel, knew her secret. Should she run? But before her fears got the best of her, a woman finally appeared from a dark alcove. Dressed in a red and gold brocade caftan, her hair covered in a headscarf that matched, she looked as exotic as the incense smelled. Elena stared. Was the gypsy real or imaginary? She wasn't sure yet.

"Is it a warrior's heart you crave? It will have to be won, *mi dulce*. He sleeps with his hand on his sword, not with a woman in his arms. He bows to his Lord, no one else."

Elena's mouth dropped open.

"His mother is in dire need and he'll go to find out what threatens her life," the woman foretold, taking a seat on a pillow on the other side of the table.

Elena sat perfectly still. The woman was so beautiful.

"Will you be his wife?" With that final question, the gypsy smiled.

Elena couldn't think clearly.

"*Mi nombre es Señora Vertina,*" she offered. "I was sent to Warwick Castle as a wedding gift for King Henry and his bride, from the king of Spain. I have time to read for you."

She held up a red velvet bag.

Elena swore she looked like an ancient sorceress from some imaginary place across the sea.

"Close your eyes," the woman instructed. "The runes will tell the truth."

Elena hesitated. She didn't have any pence in her pocket, or anything to barter with. "But . . ."

"I see *your* future. But do not ever forget, you have the power to change it. Your poor mother could not."

Elena choked back a little sob. "I'm not sure I want to know my future."

Vertina clicked her tongue, then rocked back on her heels. She smoothed the sides of her caftan. After closing her eyes, she began to take flat, polished stones out of the bag. They were not much larger than a coin, white with black lettering on one side. By the time she finished, nine lay in her hand.

Reaching across the table, she whispered, "Take these in your right hand, *por favor.*"

"Why are you whispering?"

The gypsy opened her eyes. "I respect the spirits around us. I do not wish to disturb them."

The fortuneteller looked about the tent. Then, she drew out a black satin cloth from the pouch, spreading it out on the table.

"Your mother is here. She says not to be afraid. She says be brave."

Elena bit her lower lip. She didn't like thinking about her mother, not today, not anytime. She sucked in her tears. "Aye. I'll be brave."

"*Bueno.*" The seer nodded. "Think of a question. *Si,* eyes closed. Ask the stones about James . . . his future with you, no?"

"How do you—" She stopped mid-sentence. Of course, the woman knew. Fortunetellers predicted the future. She closed her eyes, still hesitant to follow through with this. The hand she held the small stones in started shaking while she silently inquired about her future with the man she had always loved.

The gypsy's voice was barely audible now. "Elena, find the center of your spirit, the place you were born. Seek truth in the depths of your heart, then release the stones."

Feeling dizzy, Elena slowly opened her eyes. She managed to drop the runes as instructed. They made a dull sound when they hit the satin cloth. Several rolled like dice, others fell flat.

"A fine throw, *mi dulce*," Señora Vertina praised, then leaned closer.

Elena studied them. Four were in the center of the table, two face down. Two landed face up, and the remaining stones perched at the edge of the cloth.

"You know the runes?" Vertina asked.

"Aye." Elena recognized the Germanic letters. Her cousin Isabel was always at her runes. She consulted the stones before making any important decisions.

"These four," the woman said in a hushed voice, "are the most important. And these two"—she pointed—"show that you have a chance to leave Warwickshire—to embark on a journey—a great quest."

Vertina paused, flipping over the other two. "There is a member of your family who will be with you, protecting you." Her eyebrows arched.

Elena waited to hear the rest.

"Oh, *si*, of course, this stone facing down on the edge is nullified by this one. You and James can be together, but it is not certain. You must go on this journey or you will remain forever apart, never finding love."

Then the fortuneteller let out a loud sigh and stood. "You must go," she announced unexpectedly. And as quickly as she had appeared, she was gone.

Elena rubbed her eyes, then staggered to her feet. How could that woman know all her intimate secrets? Was this a ploy William had come up with to bend her to his will? She shook her head and thought better of it. The gypsy *must* be real. Hoping for a final glimpse of the woman, she looked around the tent. It was as if the fortuneteller had never been there at all.

She shrugged, too tired to care anymore. "So say the runes. I control my destiny." Then she stepped out into the world, ready to face her future.

CHAPTER 2

everything hurt, more than James wanted to admit. The fall was no different than most, but it was the unsanctioned strike to the head by his opponent's lance that left his head and one shoulder throbbing mercilessly.

He walked briskly toward the entrance to the king's stables, eager to check on his mount. Not only had he taken a savage blow, his horse may have been hurt as well, struck by Sir Hugh on the final pass.

"What? He's alive?" The shout from Sir Red caught his attention.

James nodded in greeting and joined his friend.

Red unknowingly slapped him on his damaged shoulder.

James winced from the pain shooting up his arm as if a blade had sliced it in two. But he wouldn't complain. James was a member of a small, select group of knights serving the Order of the Garter. Devoted to God, he managed the challenges that came with service to his Lord and the king through his unwavering commitment to both.

Red too was a man of brute strength, but always followed the chivalric code. Many recoiled in fear at first meeting him, his red hair and Goliath-size, but he never relied on his power unless provoked. Even though Red was a member of the Garter now, the two had once been enemies. Although those days were long behind them, James's competitive nature kept him from showing any signs of weakness.

"Good to see you, too, Brother." James ground his teeth. "Join me."

Red nodded and fell in beside him as they approached the vast stockyard. James had been here before and still found it impressive, two hundred horses were easily accommodated, if not more. James strode toward the stables.

"Will you make it a race, then?" Red asked. "What's the hurry?"

"Dragon may have been injured." It was difficult for him to hide his concern.

"Go on, man. Go see your horse. I shall meet you in the great hall later."

A grunt was James's only response as he continued on, pushing his way past a few lads carrying bales of hay on their heads. Entering the stable, he found the knight's section. Except for the soft glow of sunlight coming through the gaps between the wallboards, Dragon's stall was dark.

"'Tis all right, boy. Easy . . . easy," he soothed. "You are my champion. You performed magnificently on the field today. Although we didn't beat our foe."

He ran his hands along the horse's withers, then down to his powerful hindquarters. The steed's silky hide was dry and cool to the touch. And to his surprise, the beast looked no worse from the competition. To be sure, James bent down, then closely examined his legs. Each sported a small patch of white on the front, just above the hoof. No swelling. Relief surged through him.

"Old friend, twas a close one today," he said, standing. "I

am uncertain how Sir Hugh won. I made a direct hit and the round was a bloody draw."

The horse shook his head and whinnied. The air about the stall smelled of fresh hay. He grabbed a handful and offered it.

"We'll avenge another day."

James bowed his head for a moment. He groped for the golden cross hidden underneath his tunic, a gift from his mother on his Garter knighting day. Whenever he cheated death, he gave thanks for his mother's prayers and the good Lord's protection.

"Praise the beneficent and merciful God," he said quietly, "the Father of our Lord and Savior, Jesus Christ, for He has guarded, spared, supported, and delivered us to this hour. Let us also ask the Lord our God, to aid us in avenging our King. Amen."

"Avenge or fight, Sir James?"

Someone dared interrupt his prayer?

"You are not welcome here, sir," James snapped, turning to confront the offender. He could barely see who it was. "Show yourself."

"Sir Nicholas, Earl of Dunster. And that space is mine. You are fortunate I let your beast rest there. This is *my* property."

James frowned. "You are wrong. These stables belong to the king."

The knave still hovered in the shadows. James could discern little in the semidarkness except for Sir Nicholas's sword casing, marked with intricate engravings. The intruder gripped the weapon's handle as if he were ready to strike. But the man's ring also caught James's attention. A brilliant red stone glinted in the few threads of light left. Angry, James stepped out of the stall to size up the arrogant bastard.

"You have more important fights to wage then wagging your tongue in a stable," James taunted.

"Indeed." Sir Nicholas appeared unaffected by his words. "I take no commands from men like you." The knight's hand restlessly fingered his hilt. "I am the king's cousin. What belongs to him, belongs to me."

James greatly doubted that.

Dragon snorted and pawed the floor. But it was an approaching torch light that distracted James.

"Break it up," the man carrying the flame ordered. "We shall have no duels in the stockyards. Save it for the arena, my lords. Tis time to gather in the great hall."

With the added light, James was able to see the man who dared challenge him. Sir Nicholas was short and square. He wore a hat with a wide brim that hid his face. James was drawn to the ring on his hand. It looked familiar, but he couldn't remember where he'd seen it.

As if he knew what James was thinking, Nicholas covered his hand with a glove. "Twill be revenge when next we meet on the field," Nicholas vowed. "Mark my words." He shoved pass the guard, knocking the sentry's shoulder deliberately.

James remained silent, his mind filled with childhood memories of his home. Sir Nicholas? That was the name of the man who killed his father. God help him if they were one in the same.

* * *

AFTER LEAVING the gypsy's tent, Elena finally located William. She put her hands on her hips. "Here you are at last."

"Did I miss something?" he asked.

She glared at him.

He laughed. "Come." He hooked her arm. "Your reunion

with James could not have been that terrible. Did he bite you?" He grinned.

Unable to resist the silly notion, she laughed, too.

"Good girl. Now, let's hurry," he urged. "We don't want to miss the feast."

Elena put her frustrations aside and let her brother steer her toward the castle. Although he was a relentless teaser, she was happy to have his protection. Once they reached the castle, he guided her down the main corridor. Laughter drifted down the walkway. The celebration had already begun.

William escorted her toward the back of the opulent hall. They reached a trestle table filled with fellow squires. Trumpets blasted and a hush fell over the room. Everyone watched the royal procession. Elena hurried to a spot where she could see.

First came the beautiful ladies-in-waiting of Warwick Castle who wore golden silk tunics embroidered with the new Tudor Rose, a white bloom inside a red one. Crowned with floral wreaths woven of red and white roses, they resembled princesses.

The heralds walked behind them, their banners crisp and adorned with the king's emblem.

At last, King Henry VII and his new bride, Queen Elizabeth, drifted in, followed by the most favored lords and ladies of their court.

Everyone stood at once and deafening applause erupted. The queen glowed with pride. After nodding approvingly to the enthusiastic reception, the royal couple claimed their thrones. With an elegant wave, Her Majesty gestured all to be seated.

Servants began to bustle about the hall. Men offered pitchers of rose-scented water and towels. Overflowing baskets of fresh bread and pitchers of wine were placed on the tables.

Elena was ready for some mead after all she'd been through.

After the king's taster sampled the fair, His Royal Highness nodded to the queen. Then she raised her hand with another elegant wave, signaling the feast to begin.

Nudging her brother, Elena confessed, "I was ordered out of the tent."

"What did you expect? What kind of man do you take James for?" He laughed, raising his goblet in honor of the king.

"You tease me," she said. "I don't like it."

"What did you find, Edward?"

"A foul-mouthed, dirty warrior," she complained. "Not the sweet innocent lad I fell in love with."

William's eyes were filled with merriment. "Lads grow into men. Men become knights." He studied her face. "And what of your other goal?"

"Whatever do you mean?"

"Becoming a knight," he reminded her.

Elena gasped. The other squires stared as if they'd overheard her brother.

William chuckled, raising his cup again. "Long live the king."

The squires joined his salute.

Elena shot her brother a look of warning. How could he be so careless? Spirits. She rolled her eyes. "I admit it," she said with defiance, keeping her voice low. "I want to become a knight. I've never kept that secret from you, but we both agreed I must serve as a squire first."

Their conversation was interrupted by a woman who placed a trencher on the table in front of them.

"Peacock, venison, quail, and rabbit," the wench announced, flashing a toothless grin.

William quickly helped himself to half the meat. Always selfish, he even chose the tenderest pieces of venison.

She glowered at him. "Will nothing change? I must accept the meager portions left after you claim the best?"

He licked his fingers, then leaned in so only she could hear his reply. "To these lads you're just another squire. But I know what's underneath those pants. So yes, you are still a female, and I get the best. Be satisfied there's anything left for you to eat."

"You—" she sputtered. "Aye, you said the only way for a woman to measure a man was when he was in battle. Otherwise, you could only judge him by his groin. But I think your deplorable manners should be considered as a measure of what kind of man you are."

William laughed wickedly. "That does sound like something I would say." He scratched his chin. "Nothing has changed. Prove your commitment, renew the promise," he spoke with his mouth full. "This tournament will last a fortnight. Tis ample time for you to serve Sir James and get the needed training."

"If only our father would agree. There could be another way."

"Never," William shot back.

She ignored his words and stared out into the great hall. "I miss the days when I was allowed to spar with you. Father permitted it because you were smaller than me." She jammed her shoulder into his side.

William made a face at her. "Now *you're* the runt," he taunted. "And a chicken."

"What? Take that back," she demanded, swinging her fist. But he ducked.

He retaliated, holding one of his hands against her forehead. She tried in vain to reach him, swinging her arms wildly. No match for his strength, Elena sighed. What choice did she have? As much as she hated to admit it, serving as one of James's squires again might prove insightful.

"I accept your challenge. The vow stands." She lifted her goblet and joined her brother's toast to seal their pledge.

Setting down his cup, William smiled. He offered his right hand. "To you knighthood."

"I solemnly swear—" she started.

He gathered her small hand in his. "On our mother's grave."

Those words reminded her how seriously she must take her commitment. Swearing on her mother's soul shook her to the core. "But, Brother, I need you to—"

Another trumpet blast interrupted her. The king desired to speak.

"Welcome good servants, knights, lords, and ladies," King Henry announced. "Tonight we celebrate my marriage, the houses of Lancaster and York have been united, forming a new legacy—the House of Tudor."

Happy to be a part of the festivities, Elena was distracted by the promise she just reconfirmed. She scanned the tables for James. Where was he?

The King continued. "The War of the Roses ended weeks ago, but still there is fighting in the kingdom. Errant knights from the house of York are not willing to accept my authority."

Elena didn't mean to ignore the King, but she was intent on her own needs.

There he is.

His golden hair stood out. Even sitting down, James was a head taller than most men.

William elbowed her in the side. "Listen," he said.

"To the north, my brother, the Duke of Gloucester, is

defending the country against rebel Yorkists at Castle Berkeley. As a result, I must suspend the tournament and dispatch every one of my Garter knights and squires to aid him. I invite all to enlist. You leave tomorrow. Until then, drink and eat."

"The promise—" Elena turned to her brother.

"The matter is settled."

"You must talk to Father for me."

"Lie for you?" William's eyebrows knitted together.

Their father, Sir Guy, Earl of Warwick, had served as knight to King Richard the III. Heavily decorated, he was well revered for the support he gave to knights in the realm. Even though he had encouraged Elena to learn to ride a horse and fight alongside her brothers, he had forbidden her to leave Warwickshire to become a squire and eventually a knight. That was why William had agreed to help her get the training at the tourney.

Finally, her brother nodded. Now she wasn't sure who had the more difficult task. William would be sleeping in his comfortable feather bed.

"Where do the squires sleep?" she muttered.

"With their knights."

Elena gasped. The gypsy hadn't warned her about this. Now she could only hope for the courage to follow through with her promise.

CHAPTER 3

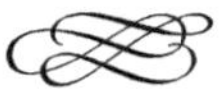

$\mathcal{E}$lena woke in the middle of the night. *Where am I?* She couldn't remember what happened. Rubbing her eyes hard, she tried to gather her thoughts. Someone was snoring dreadfully loud.

The air was damp and she smelled male sweat. She sat up and looked about. *Good Lord. The tournament tent? Oh, no. Or am I dreaming?*

She stifled a gasp when she realized who was snoring. James. A *very* naked James. Her brother had been right. Squires indeed slept alongside their knights.

Not that it bothered her much. How could she pass up what might be her only chance to see him this way? She cared little if she was acting shameless. After all, she wasn't a prude. Growing up with four brothers made her less sensitive to the male form, but *this* was different. Something stirred inside her.

Heat rose in her cheeks as she admired his naked back. The muscles and scars were fascinating. One appeared so gruesome she found it difficult to believe it hadn't crippled him. The discolored flesh began at his left shoulder and ended at his right buttock. She grimaced. Who did this? Better yet, how had he survived?

As she envisioned him being maimed by an enemy's longsword, something glittered next to him. Even from where she sat she could make out the special ornament because it was so intricately made. It was his garter, the mark of his accomplishments and honor. His sword was sheathed in a belt garnished with gold and precious jewels. She wanted to run her fingers over it, over him. Reassure him that she'd never stopped caring . . .

Upon hearing the noise of morning activities outside, she nearly cursed. No doubt squires practicing in the outer courtyard. But their voices were loud, as if they were in the tent.

James groaned as he started to roll over. Staring at his backside was one thing, catching a glimpse of his front, another. Blood pounded between her ears.

Worried he'd catch her, she grabbed her riding boots, praising God for letting him stay asleep. Whoever had put her to bed last night, thankfully left her clothed and her cap in place.

After she stood, Elena slipped on her boots. She wanted to get out of the tent, now. She wasn't ready to face James alone again.

Her hands trembled as she edged to the entrance. She turned back to admire him one last time.

"Where are you going, Edward?"

The deep voice startled her.

"My lord, I was going to get your breakfast and ready Dragon without disturbing you."

"I've already put you on notice. Going to sleep before you've fulfilled your obligations to me won't be tolerated. The dressing and undressing of your charge is a squire's duty."

She stared at the ground. Undress him? How was she going to do that? Every day? He expected her to endure that kind of torture? Impossible.

"Important people are waiting for me, boy. Dress me, now," he bellowed.

She rushed to his satchel, found his britches first, then held them out.

James stalked toward her completely naked, making her weak-kneed. When he snatched the pants, she prayed he wouldn't notice her trembling hands.

Next, she sorted through the pack again, this time looking for his leather jerkin. When she glanced up, James was staring at her with his arms crossed over his broad chest. She offered it, trying to keep her gaze focused on his face and not the rest of him. *Please no.* Any blush would give her away.

Entirely disgusted with her performance, he plucked the clothing out of her hands and tossed her an icy glare. His indifference quickly diminished the fire burning inside her heart. Elena focused on her other duties and started rolling up the pallets and packing items strewn around the shelter. She needed to keep her distance so he wouldn't discover the true nature of her sex.

"Once you're finished here, leave the packs with the stable hands, then you are dismissed." With little more than a grunt, he left.

Elena sighed with relief. She thought she was doing the right thing by agreeing to follow James, but oh, her head had opposing ideas.

Superstitious Elena believed in the runes. Surely she was destined to follow James. Traveling with him would reveal any future they had. Could she really be the master of her fate?

But the sensible Elena, struggled with the idea of

deceiving him. Was there another way for her to become a knight?

Of course there wasn't. She had explored every possibility before. That was why she was here, risking everything. But when, if ever, could she reveal the truth, that she was Elena of Warwickshire? Should she stop this charade now, before it went too far?

Craving fresh air, she tugged her cap brim low and went outside. Then she walked to the *barbican* connected with the upper bailey by a walkway. But before she could push past the entrance, she was stopped by a guard.

"Whoa, lad, hold up. State your business?"

She squared her shoulders and stretched herself to appear taller. "Sir James de Saxton of Somerset, he is my knight." She hoped her voice wouldn't crack. "I'm on my way to pledge my fealty to our king and enlist."

He eyed her. "All right, I'll let ye pass. Find Tiny Tom, he should be by the kitchen." He waved her forward.

Elena rushed into the upper bailey, anxious to get on with it. The field was already crowded. Knights flaunting family crests and squires lugging heavy regalia blocked her path.

She shoved her way through. This was no time to be timid. She began to gag before she reached the kitchen. What in God's name smelled so horrible?

She stopped abruptly and scanned the busy area. There was the cause. She stifled a scream. To her horror, three women hung from the gallows. Their feet dangled inches above the ground, but not close enough to save themselves. Hungry dogs had taken bites out of their feet already. The grotesque sight was far worse than the stench. She closed her eyes.

"Two of 'em were witches."

"What?" Elena's eyes popped open. She spun around. Who dared speak to her at such a moment?

A dwarf. He was as round as a pumpkin. A black patch covered his left eye.

"The other?" Elena asked, trying to conceal her repulsion.

"Caught stealing one 'o the king's falcons from the *mews*. They deserved what they got," he answered as if he had been the one to convict and hang them. Perhaps he was.

"Then I agree with the punishment. It was worthy of the crimes." She denounced them as convincingly as she could.

"Our king doesn't tolerate witchcraft, thievery, traitors, or liars," he assured. "No mercy in his court. *This* King of England has pledged to punish misdeeds by torture, imprisonment, or death."

"Long live our king," she declared. Then she thumped her chest like a man. "Where do the squires enlist? I'm here for Sir James de Saxton of Somerset."

"Ye found the man in charge. They call me Tiny Tom," he replied, puffing out his chest. "Jeffery, give this lad a good look over, will ye now?" he asked his companion.

Jeffery was another dwarf, who at Tom's request, stepped out of the shadows.

"Let's have a look, boy," Jeffery said. "A bit of a runt."

Elena almost giggled at the idea of the dwarf calling her a runt. She was taller and likely stronger than both of them put together.

"But I'm fast," she offered.

Jeffery's examination took longer than expected. Finally, he gave her a nod of approval. "I admit yer a small one, but I'll put you through."

Pleased, Elena bowed, then strutted across the courtyard with a newly found confidence. If she could trick those two, surely she could keep her secret from James.

Along the way, she stopped at the king's *mews*, peering into the cages. Almost all of them were empty. Most likely the birds were hunting with the master falconer or the king himself. She was reminded of Myrddin, her own bird. He went everywhere with her.

Deep in thought, she was startled when she received an unwelcome slap on the back. She whirled around to face the offender. "What do you want?"

"God's blood, *you* again?"

James. Whatever confidence she had before, disappeared instantly. But she mustered the courage to look at him. "My lord, I've enlisted," she stated proudly. "I've pledged my allegiance to you and the king."

"You enlisted for the quest?" He frowned, looking down at her. "I have no confidence in your skills. You've been released. Go, now." He strode away without giving her a chance to reply. Most of the people within earshot stared at her.

She glared at James's retreating form with disbelief. *Dismissed? Forever? No, I can't be dismissed.* She marched off in the opposite direction, angry over James's reaction. *How dare he? I'll show him.*

She reached a corner of the courtyard where the merchants were setting up stalls for the morning market. Someone tugged on her sleeve. Half expecting another slap, she spun around. "Are you not finished humiliating me?"

It wasn't James.

"Good morning Edward, you were saying?"

"What in the Lord's name are *you* doing here?"

"Helping you capture a knight," Isabel said.

Elena grabbed her cousin's arm, dragging her away so they couldn't be overheard.

"Did William put you up to this?" Elena demanded.

"My dear Edward, you have taken on a dangerous task. Her tight, blond curls bounced as she talked. "I beat the truth out of William and then *we* lied to your father." Her cousin's eyes narrowed. "I consulted my runes. They told me to come."

The gypsy. She had said a family member would join her. She had nearly forgotten that. And Isabel was the only one, other than William, who was a part of the plan.

"I advise you to take me along," Isabel continued. "I'm sworn to protect you. If it weren't for my quick thinking, you'd have been escorted home by now. Your father would not have condoned this." She gestured at Elena's appearance.

How could she deny her cousin's help? Without Isabel, she might be the only woman traveling with James.

"Now that I think upon it, I welcome the company my dear cousin," she confessed.

"'Tis settled."

"I know you'll do what you want regardless of what I say."

Isabel hugged her, igniting a reaction of whoops and hollers from the other squires nearby. Although their conversation was private, meeting in public endangered their plan. Better to pretend they were adversaries.

"Get your bloody arms off me, wretched cow," Elena screeched, pushing Isabel away. After she kicked her cousin in the shin, she spit on one of her boots. "Best figure out how you are going to get yourself assigned to this delegation."

"I'm already hired." Isabel rubbed her leg. "Cook and nurse for the Order of the Garter on the mission to Gloucestershire."

Fate. If Elena was destined to follow James, then she better figure out a way to become indispensable to him.

CHAPTER 4

The tournament tents were gone. All that remained were a crowd of sullen warriors. Although James wasn't leading them into combat, he faced a battle of wills. Would he be able to rally the knights into making the journey to Gloucestershire? Many had fought alongside him in the War of the Roses. And with the royal tournament cut short, a good number probably weren't ready for reassignment. That was the rumor.

James straightened in his saddle as he approached his brethren. He didn't waste any time getting to the point. "Fellow knights, I bid you good morn." Dragon shifted impatiently. James tightened his hold on the reins. "I know you prefer to stay here and enjoy the comforts the king's castle offers."

One of the soldiers responded with a hoot. Many laughed. James couldn't prevent his own grin. Ale and women, *that's* what all men preferred.

"Were it not for the plea from our king," he said, "I, too, would stay. I'm road-weary. But as knights, we pledge our service." He touched the medallion of St. George hanging around his neck. Their patron saint provided what protection and good fortune they needed. "Our king has chosen only those who are willing to serve."

"Aye," Red chimed in. "Remember the oath we took?" His friend knew how to rally men. "We swore homage to the Crown of England. Our duty is to the king. He will reward us handsomely when we are victorious."

Then James drew out his sword and raised it high in the air. "Who is with me?" he challenged. "Lift your weapons, those who will stop the Yorkist uprising at Berkeley Castle."

James didn't have to wait long. A sea of blades appeared. The sun reflected blindingly off their gauntlets. He counted heads. Twenty-one. That would suit him well.

"We'll ride when the sun is high over Spy Tower."

The throng cheered. James nodded appreciatively, then directed Dragon down the rocky pathway towards the stables. Red followed.

The short ride should have been uneventful, but that changed when James was threatened by an unlikely attacker.

"God's fury, take cover," James shouted. A falcon had come within inches of his head. "Here it comes again," he warned Red.

"Myrddin, return to me," a voice cried out.

Just as the falcon was about to strike again, it swerved, and whistled past James's ear. "Damn you," he shouted, reining Dragon around to confront the offender.

It was that incompetent squire. The blasted bird was perched on his shoulder. "What are you doing with one of the king's birds? Only master handlers hunt with gyrfalcons."

"Myrddin is mine. He's better trained than any of the king's birds," Edward boasted.

"That's a lie," accused a silver-haired servant who stood behind their group. "Only the king can own a gyrfalcon. Tis the law."

Edward turned to address the man. "Neither is a lie. My father is a confidant of King Henry and my bird was a gift," Edward explained calmly.

"Hand over the bird, boy," the man insisted.

When Edward refused, James came to his defense. "Why make this your affair, old man?"

"I'm the king's master falconer, Sir Robert."

James dismounted and sized him up. Sir Robert wore the royal crest on his robes and acted with the typical snobbery of anyone in close service to their monarch. Nonetheless, the lad appeared unimpressed by the falconer.

"I stand with the boy."

"We shall see about his claim," Sir Robert said, then strode across the field to a line of wired-wall sheds. He entered one, then returned a few minutes later with several items; hoods, jesses, and bells.

"Now we shall see which bird is better. You, sir"—he pointed at James—"will serve as the judge. Should the boy's falcon win, he keeps his bird. If not, he'll not only forfeit ownership, but his hands will be cut off. The punishment for owning a falcon above his station. 'Tis the law."

Edward stepped forward.

James nearly objected, but sensed Edward wanted to prove his skills. He'd pledged his allegiance to James and until now, the boy had been of little interest. He wanted to see if Edward could win.

James handed Dragon off to Red, then walked silently with the boy to the training post.

The falconer met them at the perch with an impressive hooded bird on his arm.

Edward also readied his falcon, covering Myrddin's head as instructed.

"At my signal," the man said, "you will toss two lures in

the air, then we'll call our birds. The first bird to return, wins."

James wanted to have a word with Edward to make sure he was prepared for the consequences if he lost the contest. But he was whispering to his bird, just like James did with Dragon. He'd let the boy compete.

Meat was attached to the lures and each bird sampled the prey.

Then James jogged across the field with two lures and waited for the signal to start.

Finally, the falconer dropped his raised hand, signaling James to toss them.

Wings flapped and the falcons were released. James almost cheered when Myrddin was first to take off. He watched his squire's bird fly with masterful skill, cutting off the king's falcon and taking the lead.

When Edward's bird snatched one lure with his beak and the other with his talons, James was impressed. Edward hadn't exaggerated about his bird's training.

Then the king's falcon took a detour, distracted by a pigeon, and landed on a nearby wall, seemingly no longer interested in the lures.

After a spectacular turn in the air, Myrddin swooped down with both lures, and reached the perch first, clearly the winner.

Responding to a loud whistle, the king's bird finally returned to the perch.

James laughed when Sir Robert waved a dismissive hand at Edward, then stomped off, obviously angry and ashamed over his loss.

James was pleased he'd seen his squire in action; other-wise, he would have rejected the boy. Now he had a new respect for Edward. Perhaps his small size initially made him doubt his abilities. But he had one more test for the squire.

Before James could get his attention, the lad started walking in the other direction, back toward the stables.

"Edward," he called out, embarrassed to chase a squire, but he covered the distance quickly. "Wait, boy."

The lad didn't stop. "Edward," he said again, within touching distance. He grasped his shoulder from behind. "Are you deaf, boy?" he asked, irritated. "You won."

"You doubted it, my lord?" Edward faced him.

"I was impressed with Myrddin's performance," he confessed. "You may not have been aware, but your bird blocked the other to get to both lures."

Edward chuckled. "Aye, Myrddin is well trained. It's a move he's practiced and perfected. I knew he would win."

James laughed at the boy's confidence. "You planned for your bird to cut off the other?"

"Much like a knight's skill when out maneuvering an opponent, Sir James," the boy said, his voice trailing off as if he had more to say.

"You have much to learn."

"Someone must teach me," Edward admitted. "And it must be you." Edward's gaze was intensely focused on him. "I have yet to find a champion." The boy took a deep breath. "But, my father, a former knight, has insisted I learn *his* trade, to make the sword rather than wield it. Because of this, I must enlist outside my family and prove to my father that I am worthy of knighthood. Being accepted as your squire will help me accomplish that."

Although James appreciated his situation, he wasn't sure the boy could do it. Not under his care or any other knight's. "My job is to fight," he stated plainly, "not to school lads."

"Will you never share your talent?"

"A fair question." James decided to make an offer they could both live with. "If you can complete a task before we leave, I will accept you as my squire."

Edward nodded.

"You must ride Dragon without being bucked." Something James was sure no one else could do, especially Edward.

"That's all?"

James frowned. "It's a difficult task. I'm the only one who has ever ridden the beast."

Edward appeared unmoved by his words.

"I'll be ready for my training before the sun reaches the top of Bear Tower," he said. Then the boy raced off to the stables.

* * *

ELENA WAS ECSTATIC. What a simple test, ride Dragon? If he'd asked for a kiss, it would have been more intimidating.

"Easily accomplished," she said as she entered the stable and made her way to Dragon's stall. He was the biggest horse she'd ever seen, nearly eighteen hands.

"Hello boy," she greeted him, running her fingers across his massive chest. Reaching into her pocket, she dug out an apple she'd planned to eat later.

Dragon's head snapped up and his nostrils flared.

"Shall we be friends?" she whispered, offering the treat. "I know you're as fierce as Sir James, but you have a gentle side, don't you?"

Dragon whinnied.

Elena had a special gift with animals, they trusted her and in no time, the warhorse consumed the fruit in two bites, then nuzzled her hand. She stroked his neck. With a little coaxing, she was soon seated on his back.

Grinning, she imagined riding him into battle. While other girls in her shire had dreamed of marriage and swaddling babes, she'd had loftier goals. She preferred to perfect her knife skills rather than needlepoint, and prized sword-play over sewing. She valued traits like honor and courage, instead of obedience.

Dragon snorted. She leaned down and gave the beast an affectionate pat on his neck. "I believe you're like your master." She smiled. "You both need a hard ride." She giggled, hoping she'd soon give them both what they needed.

CHAPTER 5

The sun was high in the sky when Edward came out of the royal stable riding Dragon. James couldn't believe it. The lad had accomplished the impossible.

"What have you done, boy? You cheated," he accused. "I'm the only one who has ever ridden him. This should've been beyond your ability." He eyeballed his squire. "Tell the truth, it will be easier for you in the end."

"How dare you accuse me of cheating?" The boy's face turned red.

"You couldn't have done this without help."

"You set me up for failure?"

"No, I gave you a difficult task. I wanted to measure your pluck."

"And since I've succeeded, you doubt me more?"

Whatever the blasted squire had done, it didn't feel right to James. He didn't trust anyone, especially this undersized boy. The uncomfortable silence was finally broken when Red arrived.

"What's this?" his friend asked, looking equally surprised. "Your squire has tamed Dragon."

"So it seems." James shook his head. "We were just discussing his tactics."

"Discussion?" Edward gave Red a disparaging stare. "Sir James called me a liar."

Red looked between them. "Will it come down to a bloody fist fight?" Red considered the boy. "I believe Edward. He's simply charmed Dragon."

"What?" James was stunned. "You believe him?"

"James, shall I summon the judge from the king's court?" Red twisted in the saddle, gazing toward the castle.

"I believe there's more at play here, Red, but you know I don't believe in magic." James scowled when he thought of a plausible explanation. He began to examine Dragon from head to hoof, even pushing up one of the horse's eyelids. Then he considered a plausible cause. "Now, I know how you did it. You drugged him!"

Dragon pawed at the ground.

"No," Red disagreed. "I saw for myself."

Edward sighed. "You were spying on me?"

"I've better things to do than follow a stable boy around," Red said. "It was purely accidental."

"Go on, man," urged James.

"I was looking for you. When I didn't find you in the great hall, I went to Dragon's stall and discovered the boy talking to your horse. Like you do." Red grinned broadly. "I didn't want to intrude, but when Edward climbed onto Dragon's back, I was shocked, I assure you."

James scratched his head, staring at Edward. Red wouldn't lie. As shocked as James remained, Edward deserved an apology.

"I misjudged you," he confessed, making more a statement of fact than taking blame for a mistake. But he was still stunned.

Edward exhaled some apparent frustration. "My pride is

bruised, but I will forgive you. Now you must keep your promise to train me. Teach me to become a knight." Edward dismounted.

James regretted the bet, but he had lost the wager. "God as my witness, I swear I'll train you."

Edward nodded. "Thank you, milord."

"Now," James said, "go and ready your horse, we leave at once."

* * *

As James's contingent approached the halfway mark to Gloucestershire at sunset that day, he was pleased with their progress and with Edward. The boy was an amiable companion, making the long tedious hours on the trail more bearable with his storytelling. The lad reminded him of someone . . .

Edward laughed again. The boy's eyes were filled with life and mischief.

"Once I saw an arrow pierce a knight's armored thighs, pinning him to his horse."

James chuckled. "Aye, lad, a good archer with a quick notch and a well-made arrow can pierce heavy armor. 'Tis true." He cleared his throat. It was time for training now, not fables. "But remember, as a squire, first and foremost, guard your knight. It's your duty to warn me of approaching riders. Carry your longbow at all times. Understand?"

Edward nodded.

"Treat your weapon as an extension of your body. Hold your bow in your left hand with your wrist, arm, and pointer finger in alignment. It will feel odd at first, but you'll get comfortable over time," he explained, then demonstrated. "Once the arrow is notched, draw the string until the middle finger touches the corner of your mouth, then relax the back of your hand and let the arrow fly."

Edward reached for an arrow from his quiver, then set the arrow to string as instructed. "Notch, draw, release," Edward repeated, then did as James instructed. The arrow struck the center of a tree yards away.

James grunted in approval. "Now, in order to develop the instincts of a warrior, you must practice." James raised his bow again. "Train your body to shoot accurately without aiming. When you hold your bow—"

The sound of an approaching horseman drowned out James's instructions. Lowering his weapon, he squinted into the sun. Tristan had left his post. That meant something was very wrong.

When the solider reached them, he was visibly shaken. James reigned Dragon to a stop and signaled those behind him to do the same.

Tristan rode up beside James. "Adam is down."

"Dead?"

His sentry's grim expression provided the answer he needed.

"Damn," James cursed. "I must ride ahead. Stay here and protect yourselves. We must assume we are under attack." He jammed his heels into Dragon's flanks, urging the stallion forward, eager to reach the others.

Soon he found Adam on the ground. Red was crouched beside him, examining the arrow in his chest. The rest of Tristan's regiment were still mounted, bows drawn, prepared for another attack.

"He was struck with a broad head," Red said, covering the dead knight with a cape. "He died quickly."

James swore. "Scatter. Take to brush, and see if we can ferret out the offenders, they may be the very men we've been sent to stop. I'll join the others. We'll come back for our dead brother, but first, we must capture the attackers."

James steered Dragon into the dense brush beside the trail and quickly backtracked to the other regiment, only to find them surrounded.

After dismounting, he took cover close to where his group was corralled. The men were not common thieves, but knights on horseback. The eight soldiers wore no coat of arms. For now, he'd assume they were Yorkists.

It was time for James to retaliate with a surprise attack of his own. He'd taken on larger groups alone. He readied his bow, finding and unobstructed shot at one of the marauders. Then he froze.

Blasted woman! Isabel now blocked his target, she was slumped in the saddle. Was she injured or dead? But he couldn't keep from smiling when he heard her cry out. "I have the plague." What was she about?

James moved to another hiding spot. Here he'd have a clear shot. He readied his weapon again. No, not another distraction. *Myrddin?* He'd forgotten the bird had been following them all day. What was Edward's plan?

James waited, still aiming, while the brigands backed away from the wailing Isabel. Then Myrddin took action, swooping low over the attackers, and the falcon began clawing at their helmets, distracting the errant knights.

But one of the men had his arrow fixed on the bird. Now James didn't need to wait any longer and he let his arrow fly.

The enemy archer fell from his horse, saving Edward's falcon.

"In the name of King Henry, drop your weapons or die," James ordered as he stormed out of the clearing.

The rest of the Garter knights came out from hiding, with Red in their wake. Now that both contingents had reunited, it would be easy to avenge Adam's death by killing them all, but he'd question the leader first.

"Who are you to attack the Knights of the Garter?" James demanded.

Already disarmed, the leader jumped off his horse. He tilted his chin arrogantly and glared at James. "We serve the House of York." He appeared unafraid. "We oppose any man flying the colors of Henry, that Lancastrian bastard."

This is what the king had feared. James praised God for his success. He clutched the cross at his breast, but there was more work to be done.

Red took charge, dragging the leader before James.

"Your name," James growled. He was ready to smell the bastard's traitorous blood.

"Ivan, son of the Duke of York."

"Are you a knight?" James asked.

"I follow no code."

"You do not recognize your sovereign?"

Ivan didn't hesitate when he said, "I serve no one."

"Then you'll rot in his dungeon," James promised, restraining himself from attacking even though he wanted to avenge Adam's death now.

"Red, tie him up, like the others. They'll go to prison in Gloucestershire and the king will decide their fate."

Disgusted, James turned away and walked toward the trees to get Dragon. He stopped midway when he found Edward tending his falcon.

"It's all right, Sir James killed our foe. We'll avenge another day." The boy's voice sounded angelic, almost feminine.

His squire jumped when he saw him standing there. "Sir James," the voice was deeper and more gravely than before, but a girlish blush colored his cheeks. The boy laughed nervously. "How will I ever repay you?" he choked. Tears welled up in his eyes.

James understood. It was the same with his horse. "Come, boy," he coughed, masking his own emotion. "I would expect no less from you." He squeezed the boy's shoulder. "We must be off to the nearest abbey. We've a man to bury, prayers to say, and God's grace to earn."

CHAPTER 6

So beautiful.

Until today, Elena knew of Gloucester Abbey only from her father's stories. But his tales didn't do justice to the church's true glory. Now that it was in view, she stood in absolute awe of the magnificent cathedral with its lofty ceilings and stained-glass windows. She walked through beams of color that filtered through the glass.

The beauty that surrounded her warmed her insides, reminding her of the days she spent with James. Was she falling in love *again*? Did she ever fall *out*? She must decide soon, or she'd go crazy. And with the capture of the marauders yesterday, she wondered if their mission was about to come to an early end. Once the prisoners were transferred to Berkley Castle, how many days would she have left with him?

She'd dared to meet his gaze for a brief moment yesterday after he saved her falcon. The bird meant everything to her. She had wanted to say more, but couldn't find the right words. If only she could show her appreciation. No, that would have been impossible.

Later, James had praised her quick thinking. Whenever he let down his guard, he reverted to the kinder, gentler James she'd grown to love. And if that weren't enough, they played chess last night and he let her win. *That's* the man she wanted. Now everything threatened to ruin her chances at reconnecting with him. Her disguise, his newly discovered trust in her, in Edward the squire. God's fury, she boiled inside.

The importance of her plan to receive training nearly overpowered her desire. But she'd never let her memories slip away. She'd never give up on the hope that they might have a future together. No matter what the seer predicted, or how harshly her brother dealt with her, she'd find a way to achieve all her goals. To serve and to love her knight at the same time. It was the cruelest form of torture. Whenever she felt her resolve waning, she relied on Isabel to keep her in line.

Her cousin warned if James ever found out, he would put an end to Elena's training and have her locked away forever. James wouldn't accept humiliation on any level.

The threat of his wrath wasn't enough to ease her aching heart. But there was no other choice at the moment. Squire in disguise she would remain, as long as she must. Besides, she'd dallied long enough. There were important tasks to complete. Shoving her daydreams aside, she focused on the present.

A holy man, wearing a brown robe, was busily cleaning the altar.

"Friar." She broke the silence. "My master, Sir James de Saxton of Somerset, a knight of the noblest Order of the Garter, has requested I make arrangements for the burial of one of his men."

When the friar didn't respond, she frowned and edged closer. Was he purposely ignoring her?

"Father?" She tapped his shoulder and he jumped, then turned around wearing a bewildered expression. After the initial shock wore off, he smiled warmly and pointed at his ears.

Now she understood. The poor man was deaf. He held up his hand, gesturing for her to stay, then rushed from the sanctuary.

While she waited, Elena explored the room. In a small recess just left of the main altar, she found a beautiful statue of the Virgin Mary holding Jesus. The sight of the holy pair made her regret every sin she'd ever committed, and the present deception weighed heavily on her mind. She closed her eyes.

"Oh, Lord," she whispered, "please understand why I'm doing this. You know my heart, surely you see this is for the protection of my family, for our future. I swear on my mother's soul, after I complete this mission, I'll reveal myself and embrace truth the way I always have."

After she opened her eyes, she looked around nervously, hoping no one overheard her confession. Afraid the priest would reappear at any moment, she walked back to where she was before. Minutes later, the deaf monk reappeared with another.

"Welcome to our humble abbey. I'm Friar Gregory, and this is Friar David. I'll speak for both of us. How may we help?"

Elena smiled. "I've been sent to arrange a funeral for one of my master's men." She felt guilty making such a request with no notice. "Today."

Friar Gregory regarded her quietly. "We are always at service for the men who defend our Lord."

"Thank you." Elena bowed reverently.

"The Lord has brought you to us." His kind words comforted her. "Who has fallen?"

"A knight of the Garter, killed yesterday in battle. A band of rebels, determined to defy the king, attacked us."

"Return to your master and invite him to stay with us until all the arrangements are made. We honor God's servants." The priest blessed her. "Hurry, lad."

After she left, Elena raced her palfrey along the river, passing Berkley Castle and the clearing just beyond. The camp was due south of the fortress, in a field about a league from the main gate.

Before she reached them, she slowed down. She craved time alone. Among the men, relieving herself was an embarrassing task and risky. She often made excuses to gather firewood or hunt at odd times. Elena found a densely wooded spot along the river and eyed the water. She couldn't take a full bath, but she'd wash herself. After securing her mount, she slipped out of her breeches. Then a horse whinnied, shattering her solitude.

* * *

JAMES WAS HUNTING along the river. Although he expected a banquet tomorrow at the duke's castle, he told Red he had a need for fresh rabbit. The excuse allowed him time alone with Dragon.

"Edward's a fine lad. Trustworthy, quick on his feet, he's proven me wrong," he said out loud.

Dragon whinnied.

"You agree?"

The horse snorted.

James tugged on the reins, steering Dragon left. But the animal wouldn't budge. He glanced around, looking for the cause of the horse's reaction. Then he caught sight of a tiny pale arse. James laughed, unable to look away.

"Cover your eyes," a shrill voice shouted.

"Edward?"

"Sir James?"

Dragon snorted again.

"Tis you, milord?" The boy jerked up his breeches and spun around to face him. "The friars have agreed to preside over the funeral."

The boy was clearly embarrassed. Maybe he preferred men over women? That might explain his reaction. James tried to hide his amusement. It wasn't his intention to humiliate the lad. "So the mission was successful?"

"Aye, milord."

James chuckled all the way back to camp.

Later, after gathering what they needed, James led his soldiers to Gloucester Abbey where they were welcomed with kindness and a hot meal. James would miss Adam and joined the men in celebrating his life.

After the meal was finished, Red, Tristan, and Thomas helped carry the casket containing Adam's body through the churchyard. Once they reached the gravesite, the knights formed a triangle around it.

After a hymn, Friar Gregory raised his hands. "Sir Knights, there is one sacred spot upon the earth where the footfalls of our march are not heard, the rustling of our banners have fallen silent, and the gleam of our swords don't signify victory. It's here in the place of the dead, where we now stand. Our brother Adam abides with the Lord. We loved him when he walked amongst us and now we remember him for his courage."

James sighed when the priest took the sword from the top of the coffin and presented it. "This sword endowed him with three God-like qualities—justice, fortitude, and mercy."

Then the friar pointed the blade toward heaven. "With the Lord's blessing, Adam will be touched by the sword of Divine Justice. He will join the saints and angels in the realms of light and life eternal." He offered the sword to James and bowed his head. "Let us pray."

Finished with the benediction, Friar Gregory laid a cross on the casket and it was lowered into the earth.

"What was that?" Tristan called, interrupting the final affirmation.

Edward cried out in pain.

Within seconds, James was at his squire's side, steadying him. "You are bleeding. Be still. I'm going to lay you down." He shielded him with his body. "Everyone get down. God protect us all."

CHAPTER 7

The next day, and with the Garter banner flying high, Elena followed James's warhorse through the open portcullis of Castle Berkeley.

Once inside the bailey, a rush of relief washed over her. At least for now, the danger was over. Of course, it could happen again. Men with evil ambitions wouldn't care who was killed in their efforts to thwart the new king. Her injury reminded her how vulnerable they all were.

She couldn't shake the memory of the blood on her white tunic. A few stitches from Isabel's needle made her good as new, but it could have been much worse. James had immediately come to her aide and protected her, covering her with his massive body.

Yet, he'd been close enough to discover her true identity. She prayed her secret was still safe. And by the grace of God, the arrow hadn't done more damage. If it had, she might have died in James's arms. That gave her some comfort.

Elena dismounted, then followed the group of riders across the lawn. She walked up the steps, careful not to stumble on the steep stairs.

It wasn't long before the duke's soldiers guided them down a long hallway and quickly assigned sleeping quarters, leaving James, Red, and herself for last.

James faced her once they were inside his chamber.

"You will have a respite from camp again tonight, but not from your duties," he said. "You're sleeping with me."

Elena groaned. Could she still keep up the ruse now that they'd completed the king's mission? Would she be able to endure one more night of undressing James, sleeping on a pallet next to him, and resist touching the man she loved? She ached for what she couldn't have. But her dedication hadn't failed her yet.

Red joined them in the bedchamber. "James, here are the supplies," he said, dragging canvas bags, a stool, and James's weapons to the center of the room.

Elena welcomed the company.

Red looked at her first, then James. "Give the lad a rest."

"He's a squire in training, not a helpless boy who quits whenever he gets a scratch. He stays with me." He ushered Red out of the room. Then he addressed Elena again.

"I need a bath."

So do I. Some privacy too, so she could tend to her own needs first. James was as demanding as an old woman. That made her smile.

"As *you* want," she replied. "But not as *I* wish."

"What was that?" James glanced over his shoulder at her.

She threw him an innocent look, shrugging. "Do you wish to bathe or eat first, my lord?"

"Eat." He stalked out without another word.

"Pigheaded man." Finally, time alone. Her best defense would be to go to sleep before James returned. This had served her well and kept her safe from discovery so far. Although he'd be angry, it would spare her the humiliation of seeing him naked again. The thought of bathing him made her mind spin.

With the room so warm already, memories about James nearly made it unbearable. She recalled the last time they'd been together in an intimate setting. Her childhood dreams of marrying him had never come true. Even with Isabel's assurances the fates were in her favor, she wasn't convinced.

She glanced at the enormous bed in the center of the chamber. Tempting. But the large metal tub near the hearth captured her interest more, the place where James would sit while she poured hot water over him. She couldn't do it, not dressed as his squire. But . . .

An idea popped into her mind. Without pause, she headed to the kitchen in search of a maid. After a few minutes she found one and tapped her on the shoulder. The unsuspecting servant jumped, dropping the pot she was holding.

"I'm sorry," Elena said, picking it up and handing it back to her.

"Can I help you?" the maid asked.

"Yes." Elena tried to contain her enthusiasm. "Would you bring heated water to Sir James's bedchamber?"

The girl nodded. "I have just the lads." She clapped her hands and three young boys scrambled to attention.

Satisfied her plan would be put into motion, Elena returned to the bedchamber to make further preparations. A few minutes later the door opened and the boys carried in buckets of steaming water. They poured it into the copper tub, bowed, then left.

After pinning her hair up, she undressed quickly, caring little about anything else. She deserved this small indulgence. As she submerged herself up to her shoulders, she exhaled. It was Heaven on earth. Relaxed to the point of losing herself in happy thoughts, she didn't hear the door open.

"Squire, I'm ready for my bath."

Elena gasped when she spotted James staring at her from across the room. His lips twitched. His gaze never leaving her. She folded her arms across her chest, covering her breasts, sinking deeper into the water. *My God, what have I done?* The moment she'd dreaded most had come true.

James rubbed the back of his neck, then staggered forward. "Are you a gift from the duke? Where is my bloody squire, Edward?" he growled.

He's obviously drunk more than he's eaten.

"Your squire left when I arrived to tend to your bath, milord," she answered. "He promised to return shortly." She hoped the threat of an interruption might keep James's intentions honorable.

That made him smile. "Is this how you tend to the bath for your guests?" His grin turned wicked. "A bath with you would give me great pleasure," he admitted, his heated gaze boiling her blood.

"I confess there's scarcely enough room in here for me," she warned. Yet, her observation didn't stop him from removing his boots. Then he yanked off his breeches and shirt.

Elena sucked in a nervous breath. She loved seeing him naked. But if she didn't take control of the situation soon, James would trap her in the tub.

"Come, you can sit on my lap," he suggested.

She laughed louder than she should have, uncertain of what *she* wanted. But his smoldering gaze warmed her insides, making her wonder if he didn't know who she was, what liberties she might take. She wrung her hands, unsure what to do next.

"Turn away and give me a moment of privacy, then I will tend to you." She stepped out of the tub and draped herself in a towel the boys had left.

"That arse looks familiar. This is not my first time at Berkeley, girl. Pray tell, have we been together before?"

She glanced over her shoulder. The devil hadn't turned around at all.

"No, milord. We've just met."

Blasted woods. Now she was really worried he might make the connection. But when a very naked James sauntered toward her, it cleared her mind of everything. She swallowed hard, certain she could have him right now if she so desired.

As he plopped into the tub, the water splashed her.

"You've gotten me wet," she complained.

He looked so mischievous, as if he intended to do it again. "You were already wet."

She suddenly remembered she was only wearing a towel. Now she did want to join him in the tub.

"Must I wait for my squire to do my bidding, or are you willing to risk getting wetter?" he teased.

She was certainly unafraid of a little bit of water. The wine no doubt clouded his mind. He'd never recognize her. As much as she'd worried about it, he hadn't.

"I'm at your service." She grabbed a clean linen shirt the boys had left on the bed, then walked behind a dressing screen in the room and quickly changed. Determined to please James, she then joined him by the tub, sitting on the stool next to it.

Once settled, she reached for a sponge from one of the buckets nearby and lathered it with soap. She stopped short of touching him, fascinated by his massive scar. The one she'd wondered about every time she fulfilled her squire duties.

"How did you survive the blade that left this?" She traced it with her fingers.

James laughed. "You are a curious one."

Elena's cheeks burned with embarrassment. Thank God he couldn't see the effect he had on her.

"The story of my scar is not from the battlefield, but of betrayal."

"Go on," she urged, filling the sponge with water. She'd wash it away if she could.

"A man our family once respected, Sir Nicholas Luttrell, left his mark just before he killed my father."

Her heart ached for him. She didn't know what to say, he looked so lost in thought, so filled with pain. But she had to ask the obvious question. "How did it end?"

"I was not a knight then, but still a fledgling."

"I don't understand."

"Sir Nicholas served with my father under Henry VI before the fall of the House of Lancaster. Both survived the bloody battle of Northampton together. But Nicholas came unannounced to our Cadbury home that night and accused my father of siding with the Yorkists, of committing treason."

She gasped. "Did he have proof?"

"No evidence that I've ever uncovered, but I'm determined to clear my father's name."

"Didn't your father fight?"

"I found the two alone, arguing. My father was unarmed. I tried to stop Sir Nicholas . . . to defend my father." He hung his head.

"Why do you blame yourself?" Tears welled in her eyes. She had met his father, Sir Rafe de Saxton, when he visited their home and purchased weapons from her father. She'd always believed he'd died of injuries related to battle. Dropping to her knees, she reached for his clenched jaw and turned his face towards hers. "You have always been brave."

"How would you know?"

"I'm certain you are."

He thumbed a tear off her cheek, then guided her hand

under the water. What was he doing? She dropped the sponge, her whole body went rigid.

He laughed. "You are a nervous sort. You've offered to wash me, remember? All of me."

All? With her hand firmly planted between his powerful thighs, Elena prayed for the courage to please him. At first, she wasn't sure what to do. But when he groaned with pleasure, she grew bolder, wrapping her fingers around his length, stroking. Their eyes met and he sighed, visibly enjoying her touch.

"Perhaps you could better serve me *inside* the tub." His gaze roamed over her breasts.

Willing to do whatever he wanted, she mentally prepared to join him. But a knock at the door shattered the moment.

"Go away," he shouted.

Elena took advantage of the diversion and stood, smoothing the shirt. "You are clean, milord," she said shyly. "It appears your squire has returned."

James didn't look pleased, but the interruption was a blessing. God forbid if she did something so foolish. Making love to him would expose her in so many ways. Yet desire still burned inside her. What should she do?

Red burst through the door, making the decision for her.

CHAPTER 8

*J*ames reached for his sword, but it wasn't there. How could that be? He always slept with it at his side.

"Squire," he shouted, rising from bed. Before he took a full step, he sank down. The world was spinning. God's beard, what had he done last night? The skull-splitting headache he suffered reminded him of how much he'd overindulged. And, he'd slept too long. Sunlight flooded his chamber. He rubbed the back of his neck, bits and pieces of the night's activities were coming back to him. Surely it was a dream. The woman and bath. Her sweet caresses.

The boy would explain. "Squire?" His gaze swept the room. It was empty. But the fire in the hearth appeared recently stoked. And he spotted his sword near the door.

"Edward?"

"Aye, here I am."

He appeared with a tray full of meat pies, bread, hard boiled eggs, and ham.

"Ah, squire, good to have your sturdy legs fetch my breakfast this morning. You must remember something of last night." James rubbed his eyes hard, then looked at his squire.

"What?"

The lad appeared rattled, setting the tray at the foot of the bed.

"You know I was drunk when you found me. I can't remember much of what happened last eve, tell me about the woman."

Edward stood ramrod straight. "There was a woman here?"

"I don't remember a bloody thing."

"Oh, perhaps the chambermaid? You asked me to have your bath drawn. I caught a glimpse of her when I returned and Red was leaving."

James's memory was as foggy as Edward's and he didn't like it. He groaned when he reached for a meat pie from the tray at end of the bed. Again and again James tried to conjure images of what happened. Why had he gotten so pissed?

"Did you not undress me last night?"

"No, you were naked when I returned and went to sleep right away. Did the lady hurt you, milord?"

James laughed. "Not that I recall." He rubbed his temples. "Some of it's coming back to me now."

"What can you tell me?" the boy asked with keen interest.

James studied the lad. "Have you ever *been* with a woman?"

Edward looked horrified.

His reaction made James chuckle until his stomach ached. "Do you *not* like women?"

"Nay—I mean—aye. What question did you ask first?" The boy was clearly flustered.

"Never mind, we'll find a lass for you tonight. You deserve a good tumble just like any of the boys in my service. The duke expressed his gratitude last night. I do remember that. He offered to provide food and shelter for our party as long as we wished to stay."

Instead of appearing pleased at his generous offer, Edward was beet red.

"Did you not say you needed knight's training? Not only to wield the sword, but your cock as well?"

Edward coughed. "Aye, Sir James, as you've said before, I have *much* to learn."

A hard knock sounded on the chamber door. As James stood, he stared at the boy, curious why he seemed so nervous. He knew something and James didn't like being lied to.

Edward scrambled to the door.

A guard was waiting in the corridor.

"A missive for Sir James de Saxton," the soldier announced, and handed Edward a scroll.

He delivered the parchment. James studied the wax seal. The Somerset crest, two eagle wings conjoined. He opened it and immediately recognized his stepfather's handwriting. Brief in nature, the news wasn't what he'd expected. His mother was being held for ransom.

Damn the bastards who held her captive. After his father's death, James pledged to always protect her. How could this have happened? He'd have to leave at once, and was thankful to have help. The members of the brotherhood were sworn to protect each other's families. It gave him some comfort, but not time.

"Edward, rally the knights. We have another charge. My mother, Lady Victoria, has been taken from Somerset." Grasping the cross around his neck, James stared heavenward. "God as my witness, Edward, I will not rest until I save her. Now, go."

"Aye, right away," his squire replied eagerly, then rushed out of the chamber.

Hours later James was pleased his contingent prepared so quickly. Kidnappers were an unpredictable lot. The message from his stepfather had revealed very little, making him more determined to arrive at Somerset without delay.

Under normal circumstances, the distance between Gloucestershire and Nunnery Castle took a few days, but James drove his men like a pack of wild horses, only stopping to refill their water skins. If he arrived home too late, he'd never forgive himself.

He thanked God for the fifteen knights that had agreed to join him; his squires, including Edward, and a cook. Many stayed behind, but he'd beg no man and didn't want anyone travelling with him whose heart and mind weren't fully invested in his cause. Nearing nightfall, he worried about the weary riders. They needed to stop and rest.

James reigned Dragon into a clearing, signaling the others to follow, then he addressed them. "I thank you for your allegiance. My mother means everything to me, and once I find out who kidnapped her, I will stop at nothing to deliver my vengeance. Rest for a bit, we've miles to go."

No doubt appreciative of the chance to stretch their legs and eat, the knights and squires shared a meager meal of beef jerky, oatcakes, and wine.

After the meal ended, James called Jonathan to his side. "Ready to go?" James gave his friend a weary smile.

"Aye, most are my lord, but Edward and the cook, Isabel, are still asleep. No doubt too exhausted to ride alone."

James nodded. "You take Isabel, and Edward will ride with me. We must travel quickly, time is our enemy."

Once Edward was settled in front of him, the group continued through the valley. James guarded the rear, the most vulnerable to attack.

It was still a few hours into the evening as their small contingent pushed on, but Dragon was growing restless.

"I know you're tired. When we reach Nunnery, I promise you'll rest. I've other horses that will serve in your place."

The horse whinnied.

"Now, now, jealously isn't becoming of a lady or a horse." James loved him and couldn't believe his stepfather's groomsman had nearly destroyed Dragon. The beast remained untameable until James put a saddle on his back.

Dragon whinnied again and James reached around Edward to stroke the horse's neck. But when he did, the boy tipped to one side, nearly falling. Thankfully, James caught him, pulling him back in the saddle.

"What?" James said under his breath. *A breast? By God, something is wrong here.*

He immediately withdrew his hand, grasping the boy's arm instead. Lads don't have breasts and females don't serve as squires.

Wild thoughts spun in his mind. *Who is Edward?* The feminine voice, pale skin, soft arse, it all made sense now. He had ignored his instincts when he shouldn't have. James was furious he'd been deceived.

Liars must be punished, he told himself as they crossed the drawbridge into Nunnery Castle.

CHAPTER 9

A shout from a soldier on the watch tower above startled Elena awake. It took her a moment to realize she was on Dragon with James cradling her close. She was exhausted, and her memory of the journey was foggy as their caravan crossed under the portcullis.

How did this come to be, she riding with James? Elena reached to check that her cap was still in place. Distance between them had been her best ally and now that James had begun a new quest, the deception had to continue.

With his help, she slid awkwardly from the saddle. Once her feet touched ground, her knees buckled. James steadied her.

"Thank you," she mumbled.

He grunted, staring at her in a way she didn't know how to interpret.

What is he thinking?

She breathed a sigh of relief when he walked away and started barking orders at his men.

Her cheeks burned when she remembered their last encounter, before he'd found out his mother was missing.

Moments later, she cringed when he screamed her name, the entire courtyard starring at her. Not knowing what else to do, she followed him inside the keep.

"You are earlier than expected," a nobleman announced, greeting them with a courtyard full of servants behind him. "You must have traveled without much rest," he said, offering nothing more.

"Did we interrupt a formal proceeding, Duke?" James asked.

So this proud man was Sir Richard Fairfaux, the Duke of Somerset. He was at least a foot shorter than James. Dressed in regal robes, he sported long, silver hair and a well-groomed beard, but wore an expression of dread.

"I'm preparing to collect the aids taxes, the funds for the ransom," the nobleman answered.

Elena couldn't believe how cold James's stepfather sounded. Was he raising funds to save his wife or conducting business?

"Tell me of my mother," James said. "What news?"

"'Tis believed she's been captured by Yorkists." His stepfather clapped his hands, dismissing the servants. He leaned closer. "There's still much unrest here."

"What are the demands?" Veins strained in James's neck.

"A joust *et nex*," the duke replied.

"To the death? Why collect monies then?" James clenched his hands at his sides.

"I have little patience with outlaws," Richard answered. "I prefer a payment instead of meeting their bloody terms."

"You will not trifle with my mother's life." James stepped forward, towering over his stepfather, his anger seeping from every pore. "Tell me who was named in this dual."

Richard took a step backward.

"You."

Elena gasped.

James glared at her.

" . . . and Sir Nicholas Luttrell, the reinstated Earl of Dunster."

Elena struggled to control her emotions. Sir Nicholas, the man James hated more than any other? There was no question what her knight would do.

"I must fight. 'Tis part of the oath I took."

"I expected as much, but I'm preparing for a contingency. I sent a missive today to Sir Nicholas with my offer."

"God's blood," James shouted, stepping toe to toe with the duke. He leaned down and pressed his forehead against Richard's. "Sixteen long years I've waited to avenge my father's death. Now I have the chance. What knight would not act upon that?"

Sir Richard made no attempt to move away when he answered his stepson. "This is why I sought another resolution."

"Cowards shun duty." James shoved the duke away and spit on the ground by his feet. "You've never faced battle. Your family has always relied on the service of knights they paid for protection. If you knew my grandfather, my father, or me—all who served the Order—you would not question my motives or abilities."

"With so much at stake, I don't believe you can beat the bastard," argued the duke. "He comes from a family of tyrannous men. His grandfather, Sir James Luttrell committed treason under Henry the IV."

James glared at his stepfather.

But the duke had more to say as he closed the distance between them.

"He lived a cruel life, subjecting many to his terror. He also murdered the Duke of York at Wakefield and was convicted of high treason. Sir Nicholas's grandfather forfeited all the family's estates to King Edward.

"Now King Henry has returned all their properties. The Luttrell family and Sir Nicholas are in good favor once again. Nicholas has reclaimed Dunster Castle and his title. It wouldn't be wise to fight him."

"So it was the same Sir Nicholas at Warwick?" James asked, his temper appearing to cool.

"The same?" His stepfather looked puzzled.

"'Tis of no importance." James waved him off and began to pace. "Have you seen Sir Nicholas in recent days?"

"No one here has seen him, but it's rumored he left Fyvie Castle in Scotland. I've heard tell he wears many disguises."

"What you've said doesn't change the truth. The man murdered my father. I thought Sir Nicholas dead, but I must be certain of it. I'll fight this villain for more reasons than you need to know."

The duke paced a hand on James's shoulder and his expression softened. "Trust I love Victoria, too. Her safe return is all I can think about. We have that in common."

James gave the duke a curt nod, then bowed his head in apparent resolution.

Sir Richard clapped his hands. "I shall make the necessary preparations for a joust."

Elena wanted to cry out in protest. She understood why James wanted Sir Nicholas dead, but hoped there was another way to save his mother.

THE LUTTRELL SEAL was still soft on the scroll when Nicholas handed it to his herald. It was his reply to the Duke of Somerset who had asked to pay a ransom instead of fulfilling his demand for a joust. Nicholas didn't care what the duke wanted.

He held his wife prisoner here in Cadbury Castle. The

same stronghold where he'd slaughtered her first husband and scarred her son with his sword. Land was his ambition. And he'd do anything to get it.

Wisely, he'd kept out of Victoria's sight. She'd dealt with his servants who fed her scraps of food, just enough to keep the bitch alive. But now that her son James, a Garter knight, had returned to Somerset, it was time to visit her in the tower.

Nicholas arrived at her cell and peered through the barred window. She was sleeping on a pallet on the floor. He unlocked the door and went inside.

"Get up," he called out. She didn't move. "Victoria, your husband has sent a messenger. The duke is anxious for your return and is willing to pay a fine ransom, five hundred pieces of gold." He sneered at her. "He prays for your swift return."

Rising up on all fours, she snarled at him like a lioness. She was still beautiful, with gold hair down to her waist and startling blue eyes.

"Bastard! Your men would not confirm it when I asked, but I suspected it was you behind this treachery. Release me," she demanded. "The new king will have your head, I promise."

"Your ignorance is refreshing."

She considered him for a moment. "Tis a generous offer. You must be tempted," she taunted.

"Tis blood and land I want," he answered. "Nothing else matters. Not even *your* life."

"Blood is your ambition. Why have you left Scotland? This castle is not your domain. You've been banned from England."

Even deprived of food and comforts, the woman still had the spirit to fight.

"There was more than Fyvie in the marriage contract. Ask

your mother, she will confirm it." He laughed wickedly at her shocked expression. "Indeed, I'm quite comfortable here."

"Why now?" she cried. "After James joined the Order and we were married in secret, you promised to stay in Scotland. That was the agreement."

"Victoria, there is a new king. Lest you forget, he is my cousin. I have reclaimed Dunster Castle. I'll have more power over the realm and—"

"Dunster Castle?" She cut him off. "Your family was found guilty of treason, you have no holdings, no rights."

He furrowed his brow. "Twas many years ago. I've received the king's pardon. Dunster, Cadbury, and Fyvie are mine. You forfeited your land when you married me." He laughed. "Who are you to throw stones? You're a bigamist in the eyes of God and the king."

"May God curse you," she cried out, grabbing the cell bars. "Our marriage was a lie. You coerced me with fear. I know that now."

Ignoring her curses, he left, ready to prepare for a joust *et nex*.

CHAPTER 10

$\mathcal{E}$lena was escorted to her own bedchamber after the evening meal. It was a beautiful refuge from what had become familiar to her, sleeping on the ground next to James. The space reminded her of home. She missed her family, even William.

She appreciated that her knight had agreed to let her sleep alone tonight. If he hadn't, she wasn't sure she could have controlled herself. Not after the bath at Berkley Castle. Although she'd climbed into his bed after he'd fallen asleep and left early so he wouldn't find her next to him in the morning, she still knew where she really wanted to be.

Elena sighed and punched the pillow, then rolled over. She was exhausted, but couldn't sleep. Maybe a walk would help. She scooted out of bed and slipped her breeches on under her nightshirt. Draping her cloak around her shoulders, she headed downstairs. But before she rounded the corner, someone grabbed her.

"Squire, who are you stalking at this late hour?" James asked.

"I couldn't sleep."

"Come to my chamber."

Elena didn't know what to think.

"Squire!"

"Coming, milord." She scrambled after him. But when Elena entered his room, she gasped when he greeted her with the tip of his sword.

"Come in, *Edward*. Is that your given name?" He circled around her, then bolted the door. "Undress," he ordered.

"My lord, I do not understand."

"It's a simple request. If you find it too difficult, I'll assist you." He started toward her.

"I can explain." She backed away, intent on protecting her identity, determined to keep his hands off her. Panic ravaged her body. Did he know everything? She was trapped and if she couldn't escape, she'd be forced to reveal her secret.

"Undress, *now*."

Very slowly, Elena did as he demanded. First her tunic, then her breeches. Standing naked and helpless before him, she prayed for strength and his mercy. She folded her arms over her breasts, shielding herself from his piercing gaze.

"Satan's work," he hissed. "You lied to me, Edward. Everything you said and did. I trusted you." He sounded so disappointed and looked so angry.

"Isn't this what you expected?" she yelled. "Don't you recognize me now? Or are you too drunk to see clearly? I'm Elena of Warwickshire. My father was a famous knight. You must remember me." She was quivering, overcome by emotions.

James was breathing hard as he turned away, staring at the fire in the hearth. She could hear him muttering and cursing. When he whirled around again, the look on his face nearly made her faint.

Oh God, what can I do?

He stalked toward her.

"Don't hurt me," she pleaded, grabbing her squire's shirt and covering herself.

He stopped and seethed his sword, his expression softening.

Summoning what courage she had left, she spoke quietly. "You saved my life. Do you remember when I fell from the tree? You carried me home."

It almost seemed to take forever for him to respond until he finally said, "You took a hard fall."

"You *do* remember." Without hesitation, she jumped into his arms, wrapping her legs around him, holding on tight.

"Elli, I left for the Order before you recovered. You were asleep for weeks. I was sure you died," he confessed, cupping her cheek. Then he paused as if having trouble remembering. "But you were promised to Sir Thomas. Didn't you marry him?"

She shook her head.

"Or are you a widow?"

"Nay," she whimpered, wanting to forget the heartbreak she'd endured when he left for the Garter and had not returned for her.

"Then I've found you again, Elli. But you've lied to me. For days at a time." He dislodged her, setting her on her feet. "I cannot forget or forgive that." He raked his hands through his hair, then paced the room.

"I lied to serve you. To learn from you. To be close to you again. Is it a sin to aspire to become an honored knight like you?" For some unknown reason she was no longer afraid and straightened her shoulders, holding herself with pride. "If I'd asked to be your squire, come to you as Elena of Warwickshire, you would've denied me. My brother, William, convinced me to dress as a boy."

Icy blue eyes met hers. Not a hint of warmth or emotion

showed in their depths. He was clearly troubled by her confession. He came at her, stopping inches away.

"I am sorry for deceiving you, Sir James." She twisted her hands together nervously, waiting for a response.

"I remember you wanted to become a knight to avoid marrying Thomas, but I told you women are forbidden from service." His eyes didn't leave hers. "Do you care about me?" he whispered, then brushed a kiss across her cheek.

There was only one way to find out. Her nipples hardened as she stepped closer to him, pressing her body against his. At first his arms hung at his sides, but when she embraced him, grinding her hips against him, he hugged her tight and moaned.

"You make a better girl, Elena." His warm breath tickled her skin. "You've become a beautiful woman, but a dishonest one."

His words stung, but all she cared about was running her hands over his hard body, feeling the man she'd loved and desired for so long.

"I've some confessions of mine own." He let go and sat on the edge of the bed, inviting her to join him with a gesture. "You need to know."

She accepted his invitation, leaning against him, wanting to steal his warmth.

"I should punish you," he said. "But I'm not a heartless man. There's one thing you must understand, I can never marry. I've taken vows."

The news saddened her. Cold crept through her body, nearly extinguishing the flame in her heart.

He picked up a fur and draped it across her shoulders. "It seems your efforts have been a waste of time. I'm honoring a wish my mother made, too. When I chose the Garter, I did so to serve the king and her."

"Why would a mother wish her son never to marry?

Why?" She gasped and covered her face, tears burning her eyes.

"It matters not. I spoke my vows." He gently removed her hands from her face so he could see her eyes.

"Elli, I once loved you," he confessed. "I asked you to wait for me, even though I knew you were promised to another. Instead of returning to you, I dedicated myself to God and the king."

"You loved me?"

"I was young and I didn't know anything about love. I had no right to ask you to wait," he admitted, but the longing and desire in his eyes didn't match his words. "Whatever we share can never end in marriage. For the protection of your honor, learn to be a knight. Forget everything else."

Frustrated and embarrassed, Elena gathered the rest of her clothing from the floor. She hid her face as she dressed, wishing she could escape.

"Training is all we'll ever share?"

"Aye," he said in an icy tone.

She glanced at him over her shoulder. "James?" Her mind said one thing, her heart another.

"Return to your chambers, *squire*."

She had her answer. James was no longer the boy she had fallen in love with. As she left his room, she realized her dream of marrying him was gone forever. The runes were wrong. Any future with James was impossible.

CHAPTER 11

hen Elena left early the next morning with
Isabel and Tristan, on a mission to Glaston-
bury Abbey, James had been distant. Other than a brief repri-
mand and his agreement to let her remain in disguise, he
refused to speak to her afterward.

Elena shrugged Myrddin off her shoulder, then gripped
her reigns tighter, turning her attention to Isabel who sat on
the bench beside her. Another wagon trailed after them,
carrying barrels full of wine that would be served at the
Lenten fest that evening.

Elena was grateful her cousin had agreed to continue on
the Garter knight retinue, now with the mission to save
James's mother. But as they finally had time alone together,
she expected Isabell to insist they return home after the
Lenten.

"You are naïve, Elena, if you expected a proposal from
James after deceiving him." Isabel was clearly siding with him
and that wasn't helping. "He's no fool." Her cousin gave her a
disgusted look.

"He may *never* forgive me. I realize that now. *I'm* the fool."

Tears trickled down her face, but she quickly swiped them away. Devastated by James's confession last night, she had hoped to gain a sympathetic ear from Isabel.

"Remember when I threw the runes at Castle Berkley, I told you it was time to reveal your secret to him."

"I know," Elena admitted. She hadn't been completely honest with Isabel then. After she had pretended to be a maid, she was afraid of further consequences. Lying more than once to James about who she was had complicated matters even more. For now, that truth resided only with her.

A disruption of approaching horses stopped Elena's further pleas for understanding. Glancing over her shoulder, she found a group of knights, wearing the king's colors, about to overtake them. Expecting them to pass peacefully, she slowed as they approached. But instead of a cordial greeting, they drove their horses in front of the wagon and blocked her path.

"Halt. Now."

It took all of Elena's strength to stop the wagon.

"We have been ordered to arrest anyone who trespasses here," the captain informed them.

Before Elena could gather her thoughts to address the knights, their escort rode up beside them.

"I'm Tristan of the Garter." He spoke with the authority she lacked. "What is the charge?"

"Unlawful hunting," the captain answered. "We were following your party. Your falcon is looking for prey."

"There is no falcon in our party." Tristan stated what he believed to be true. Yet, ever since she had defied custom and joined James's crusade, she had been under Myrddin's watchful eye.

"Kill the bird," the leader ordered.

"No," Elena cried. "He's mine. Don't kill him." She'd do

anything to protect her falcon. "I am from Warwickshire and ignorant of the laws of the king."

"'Tis no excuse." One of the soldiers dismounted and approached the wagon.

Tristan blocked his path with his horse. "This squire serves James of Somerset, the duke's son. He should be answerable for the charge."

Fearing James more than prison, Elena objected. "No, I'm of age. Spare the bird. I will go." Elena gave Isabel a pleading glance.

Her cousin paled. But Elena handed the reins to her.

Tristan helped Elena from the bench. A soldier tied her hands together, then lifted her onto her horse, Windogger, who'd been tied to the back of the waggon.

As she rode way with the regiment, she glanced back at Isabel. Whatever trouble awaited her, she was ready.

* * *

WHILE A PARADE of servants carried in steaming trenchers of Lenten vegetable stew, James scanned the tables for Elena. He had decided to allow her to remain in her disguise. It had taken every ounce of control not to give in to his urges last night. Not to grab her like a possessive Viking lord, then carry her to his bed like a prize.

Elli. He hadn't forgotten her and on lonely nights, she had haunted his dreams. Of course he'd thought she'd be married by now, with children. Even though he was thrilled she was not someone else's wife, he was tortured by the circumstances. His promise never to marry and her lies. The first, he had to keep. The other, he could not accept.

When the food was set before him, vegetables colored with herbs, he grunted his disapproval. Within the Lenten, he was to have no meat until Easter. He loved his Lord, but a knight needed sustenance, no matter what the day. If only his squire were here to distract him. Surely, she should be back from the abbey by now.

"My lord, we are serving the pretzel tonight," a pretty, young servant offered.

He grabbed a piece from the platter, but even her smile did not brighten his mood. Instead, he glared at the servant.

Where is my squire?

He was relieved when Tristan finally entered the great hall. His second in command would know of his squire's whereabouts. He waved the man over.

"Where is my squire?"

"I sent word, my lord," Tristan said.

"When?"

"Did you not hear?"

"Who was to deliver it?"

"The cook, Isabel."

"Out with it, man," he demanded.

"The king's soldiers took Edward."

James pounded his fist on the table. "And you allowed it?"

"It was the falcon."

His patience gone. "Where is he?"

Tristan's eyes filled with dread. "In Somerset prison," he said at last.

James stood up, knocking over his chair. The duke and the other nobles stopped their conversation, but he didn't care. Ignoring Richard's questioning and the gasps from the high table, he brushed past Tristan, then strode purposefully through the great hall. There was only one thing he could do now. Rescue his squire.

During his brief ride from the duke's fortress, the prospect of punishing Elena, after she was in his custody, was all that had kept him sane until he entered the small village.

When he arrived at the prison entry, his insides were boiling. After dismounting and securing Dragon, he pounded his shield against the door while he prayed they hadn't tortured her, or worse. He shuddered at the thought.

A sentry finally opened the small peep hole in the metal door.

"Who is it?" the guard asked.

"James of Somerset, Knight of the Garter, servant to King Henry the VII." A mutton-headed guard was not going to slow his progress. "As the king's servant I command you, let me pass."

The man grunted and shuffled around.

Red should have joined James, but he'd rushed out of the great hall hell bent on rescuing his squire. Not the lad Edward, but a lady. He had yet to tell anyone her secret, not even Red.

At last, the door swung open. The torch inside the gate lit enough of the entryway so he could make out the three crowns of England and the forester symbol of a tree branch on their surcoats.

"State your purpose," growled one of the guards.

"Here to retrieve my property. One squire, Edward of Warwickshire, unjustly taken."

"Follow me," the guard ordered.

He was escorted into the prison down a dim, narrow corridor, passing empty cells along the way.

"What is the charge?" James demanded.

The guard ignored James.

"Are you deaf man, what is the charge?" he asked again, grabbing the soldier and turning him around.

"Hunting without a permit. Your squire was caught with a falcon and bow."

James took a deep breath. Just because Elena possessed a falcon and bow didn't mean she was necessarily hunting. "As the heir to the Duke of Somerset, I'm granted one deer a year, especially in the holy season. Do you not know the laws?"

"I'm here to enforce the law."

"Do you deny my claim?" James asked, towering over the king's servant. "Just because the lad had a bird and weapon doesn't mean he was hunting, he was acting on my orders to protect my guests."

The soldier rubbed his chin. "The law entitles the duke to hunt in the presence of a forester." The man stepped back. "As for your other excuse, I know what I was told, your squire was hunting."

James sighed, there was no use arguing. "What is the fine?"

"A male horse."

"What?" James swore to himself. "The fines have always been paid in marks."

"The forester has the right to determine the penalty."

"James, don't do it. They have Windogger." Elena's voice as Edward echoed down the corridor. "Let me rot in here. I deserve it."

Aye, she does, but I won't let that happen.

"Edward, it is my bidding you must do," he shouted back. Elena had been more compliant as a lad. *Damn that woman.*

But he knew the only way to get her back was to comply with the forester's demand. Elena's horse was a mare. The greedy guard had seen Dragon, the best piece of male horse-flesh in all of England.

"Free my squire. My warhorse is yours to keep."

CHAPTER 12

The journey back to the castle proved to be more torturous for Elena than the prison cell. She sensed James's displeasure as she rode behind him on Windogger. She dared not touch him, though she wanted to.

Elena had prayed that he would rescue her, but not at the price he paid. How would she ever make this right? First, she'd lost his trust. Now he'd lost Dragon because of her carelessness. She fully expected to be escorted back to Warwickshire after they returned to Nunnery. She hoped it would be with anyone but James or she wouldn't survive it.

"God's blood, woman, who do you think you are?" His deep, powerful voice made her cringe.

She couldn't answer.

He sighed, steering the horse underneath some trees. Then he turned so abruptly, she thought he'd strike her. "Are you daft, woman?"

She covered her face with both hands.

"You're not ready to be a knight, Elena. Look at me." He drew her hands away. "You've sworn allegiance to me, but you constantly disobey." His eyebrows knit together. "You've begged for guidance, yet refuse to follow my instructions." He shook his head. "You speak of courage, yet don't show any. Did you not consider the consequences when you lied your way into my life? You're selfish and don't consider the future. The ability to sacrifice for the good of others is what qualifies a man for knighthood. Your heart is unworthy."

But her heart *was* worthy. Perhaps not for knighthood, but for love. His love. And that seemed more important to her now. Although his criticism hurt, she knew he cared about her. His eyes showed it.

Giving in to her urges, she leaned against him. Her quivering lips met his. This was the only answer she could give. She needed to sate her unbridled passion. She wanted him. She wanted this. It might be her only chance before he came to his senses.

He responded, embracing her.

When he finally released her, she whimpered and leaned into him, wanting more.

He gazed into her eyes. Why had he stopped?

"Elli. This is not right."

All she could feel was the thundering of her heart. She leaned forward, intending to kiss him again.

"No, Elena." He removed her hands from around his neck. "I cannot. I won't dishonor you or myself. You and I can never be together. Don't you understand?"

She hung her head.

"Never, Elena. Never. We'll go home now."

The connection was broken. Cold whirled around her once more.

Never, Elena. His words echoed in her mind. Her quest had ended.

.   .   .

No more than an hour after the silent ride home and she was safely returned to Nunnery Castle, James left her alone. Asking God for guidance, Elena changed into a traveling dress and cape, then went to the mews where her falcon was kept.

"Come, Myrddin, you'll have a new home before the sun sets, with a new master."

Then she saddled Winddogger and rode back to the prison. Numb to her emotions, she was determined to earn James's trust again as she traveled. Only this great sacrifice might make it right.

After she arrived at the entry and knocked, the sentry greeted her coldly.

"I'm here to see the captain who arrested me."

Without any further words between them, the guard escorted her down a corridor, then directed her into a room with a table and chairs.

"Explain your return," a man asked, one she couldn't see.

"I'm here to offer a trade."

"We do not barter with women."

Elena rolled her eyes. "I believe I have something you'd like."

"How would a scrawny girl know what I enjoy?" A man of notable wealth stepped from the shadows. He wasn't a soldier, but a man of consequence. His clothes were made of the finest fabrics. "I serve the king *and* myself."

"I meant no offense, milord."

He gawked at her, his dark gaze sliding up her body. Truly, this man frightened her.

"Please, let me speak," she insisted.

He rubbed his chin. "What do you have to trade?" He edged closer.

Elena stepped back. Chewing on her lower lip, she regretted presenting herself as a female. This egotistical man wanted special favors, she could see it in his eyes. She pulled her cloak tighter around her body, hoping to block his view. "I have an exceptional falcon, worth more than any horse."

His eyes narrowed, then he laughed. "No bird is worth more than a warhorse." He turned to go.

"I'll also give you my horse and my services."

The noble spun back around. "Your services?" He repeated, making it sound sinful.

Her heart raced. "As an escort," she explained.

He laughed again. "There's hundreds of women at my disposal who offer much more."

"Please," she begged. "I have nothing else to give."

The man waved his hand and Elena eyed the ring on his finger. A dragon's tail wrapped around a red stone?

Noticing her interest, he covered his hand.

"I will guarantee your admittance to the joust this coming week—a fight to the death."

"To the death?"

"A well-guarded secret." She lowered her voice, afraid someone might overhear. "James of Somerset has been challenged to fight to free his mother. He'll face Sir Nicholas, a man he despises."

"Sir Nicholas from the notorious Luttrell family?" the stranger asked. "I know of him." He sounded intrigued.

"You'll attend the event as my personal guest," she assured him. "I promise you won't be disappointed."

"How could I be?" he asked. "I'd pay a fair share of gold to witness such a contest." He grinned. "Agreed. Your falcon, horse, and *services*."

CHAPTER 13

"Where is my squire?" James demanded, bursting into the kitchen.

Isabel scooped some white stones off the scarred, wooden table and thrust them into a pouch. He refused to be ignored again, by anyone. He'd get her blasted attention.

"Are you deaf, woman?" he shouted as if she was. "Where's that devil?"

"Curse you," Isabel screeched, coming at him and James scooted out of her path.

She picked up a meat hook and shook it at him. "Out of my kitchen."

James considered reprimanding her in front of the other servants for her disrespect, but she was Elena's cousin. A fact he'd just discovered from Tristan earlier that morning.

He decided to look for Red. He wasn't getting any help here.

It only took a few moments to reach the lower bailey, where he found his men-at-arms at sword play. Red stood at the quintain. Many were leveled by the dummy fashioned of mail. Once struck, the device could unseat a rider if he didn't get past it quickly enough.

Red greeted him. "There you are. Slept late?"

James wasn't in the mood for friendly banter. "How goes the training?"

"Few stayed in the saddle, even after several tries. None of them are worthy of jousting. We have work to do."

James nodded. "But will they be ready to squire?"

"Aye." He grinned, as confident as always.

"Are you certain Edward is ready?" That was really all James cared about.

As much as he wanted to trust Elena, now that he knew who she was, he had his doubts. Soon, he'd tell Red about his proposal to her, the one he ran away from, but he'd promised to keep that truth and her disguise secret for now.

"Of course. He's the best of the lot," another man answered, approaching from behind. James recognized that voice.

"God's blood," he shouted, spinning around. "How is it that Dragon has returned? Are you a wizard or a squire? For only a spell could have conjured my horse."

"A negotiation, not magic," Elena said.

James grunted and stared up at her. She shifted in the saddle, looking uncomfortable. Good. She deserved to squirm after all she'd put him through.

Red eyeballed Edward. "Are you prepared for the contest?"

"If I could take James's place, I would," she replied somberly.

James snorted and grabbed Dragon's bridle. He nuzzled close to the beast's nose. *Why does this woman test my patience and challenge my knightly oaths? What to do with her?*

"A word with you, Red," she said, dismounting. "It's unlikely I'll attend the joust," she whispered, keeping her distance from James. "Will you consider escorting Isabel and I to Warwickshire? We would—"

"Have you turned coward, boy?" James roared. How dare she? "After all my efforts, you'd abandon your post just before the contest?"

"Not my wish, but—"

"Squires aren't granted wishes." James ignored the curious glances from around the courtyard. "Are you willing to break a solemn vow? If you want to leave, you must win your freedom."

She glared at him, her eyes sparking. For a moment, he thought she'd run. Instead, she strode forward, fingering the hilt of her sword.

James handed Dragon's reins to Red, then stepped even closer to her. "Edward, only a coward would retreat."

"You're calling me a coward?" Elena gave him a threatening look.

"If you break vows, you are."

"I'm prepared to fight. Draw your weapon," she challenged. "I don't intend to take you down unarmed." She threw back her head, and when her gaze met his, she didn't look frightened any more.

"I'll face Edward," shouted a squire.

"Choose me, milord," volunteered another.

"My student. My fight." James squared his shoulders. After he unsheathed his longsword, he drew a line in the dirt with the heel of his boot.

"No lesson required today, milord," Elena boasted. She shifted on her feet. "Prepare yourself."

She makes this easy. I'll let her exhaust herself.

Still standing behind the line, James waited for her to advance. She circled him, moving to her right first, her sword braced in both hands.

James mirrored her movements.

"We aren't equals," James taunted. "I'll fight with my weaker hand. You'll need both for your efforts." *If she's angry, she'll lose focus.*

"No need to give me an advantage. For when I win, and I shall, it must be considered a fair contest."

"If you wish," he conceded, switching his sword to his dominate side.

That was when Elena struck. She cut her sword over his, with the skill of a man, and knocked it from his hands. Shocked and surprised to see his longsword lying in the dirt, James swore under his breath. His gaze met hers again, and he was unprepared for her arrogant smirk.

"A primitive move," he said, lowering his head as if to concede. "But effective."

He drew an ax from his belt and lunged at her. He easily knocked her sword out of her hands. With a laugh, he held his weapon to her throat.

"Still your student," she mumbled, accepting the loss.

"Still my squire." Then he pressed something into her hand. "Your next training session will be in my trophy room. Now go."

* * *

ELENA LOWERED her head to hide her embarrassment. Although her pride was bruised, she was thankful he'd fought to keep her. After crossing the bailey and reaching the main entry of the castle, she climbed the stairs two at a time, anxious to reach the trophy room. Once inside, her anger was replaced by curiosity. This room, adjacent to James's bedchamber, had remained forbidden.

At first, her gaze was drawn to a banner on the far wall. It featured the Garter's patron, Saint George, slaying a dragon. She read the Latin words out loud, *honi soit qui mal y pense.*

The Garter's motto. James had told her what it meant: Shame upon him who thinks evil upon it.

She explored the rest of the space. There was a massive bed with two battered swords crossed at the center, fashioned into a headboard.

A wall of shields framed the door. Each displayed the cross of Saint George with a small plaque that marked the year and battle. James's history was before her eyes.

Not wanting to wait until he joined her to read the shields more closely, she dragged a small chest over to the wall. She was just climbing up when he entered the room, slamming the door and knocking her off balance.

She fell into his arms.

"Praise God I caught you." He chuckled. "What mischief are you up to?"

Memories flooded her mind, him carrying her after she'd fallen from the tree. His gaze suggested nothing but adoration, and the way he held her so close. . . It gave her hope. Perhaps there was a way to chip away at his resolve to stay apart, to make him love her again.

"Elli?"

She pushed her thoughts aside. "I'm admiring my lord's accomplishments."

He smiled. "Aye, my many battles. My mother built this shrine, a living memorial to me. Want a closer look?"

She squealed when he grabbed her about the waist, then hoisted her onto his shoulders. She held the top of his head to keep balance. They'd played these sort of games in the woods together when they were young, wrestling and play fighting.

But Elena was determined to keep her feelings hidden. She listened closely to his stories. Now she understood how her knight had become so shrewd and honored, so scarred and brutal. He'd also escaped many brushes with death, outwitting his enemies and gaining prestige.

Once he finished speaking, he turned from the wall and unsheathed his beloved sword. He held it up, offering her the handle.

"Take it."

"You honor me." She held it aloft, admiring the hammered steel.

"Do you remember the time we spent together?" he asked.

James couldn't know how often she relived those sweet memories. He'd influenced her more than anyone. The reason why she wanted to be a knight. In the absence of a mother or any other notable female influences, she'd grown up learning to fight with her fists and weapons.

"Games? I thought they were real," she answered, laughing. "Shall we relive those moments now?"

He snorted like a horse in response. "All right. You are the noble knight, Elena of Warwickshire, and I, your warhorse. You have accepted a challenge to fight the feared Sir Nicholas to the death. The arena is filled with spectators shouting your name. Some will salute you, others will wish you dead. Now, be at the ready."

She nodded.

"You are approaching the ring and searching for your squire, Edward. Where's the lad? Is he sleeping or just a lazy boy with no intention to honor his word?"

She wouldn't tolerate his insults. "There he is, tending the injured Sir James who cannot stand without the assistance of his squires."

A knock sounded on the door. Neither of them moved.

After a second knock, Red stepped inside. He looked confused. "I thought you'd be here alone." He stared up at Elena, then back at James.

"Go on," James insisted.

Red shook his head, perhaps wanting to say something about the awkward position he'd caught them in. "I spoke with a member of your stepfather's guard who fought Sir Nicholas at Warwickshire, at the king's tourney."

James exhaled. "Anything about that bastard interests me. I will join you shortly."

Red bowed his head, then departed.

"I'm afraid our time together has ended," James said. "Sir Nicholas has postponed the match until tomorrow." He walked over to the bed. "Return my sword, vixen."

She carefully lowered it. Once it was safely sheathed, he dropped her onto his bed.

"Why did you do that?"

"This is where I expect you to stay until I return. And if you disagree, I'll tie you to the blasted headboard. Understand?"

She studied him closely. She didn't doubt the threat, but she'd never stay. "Yes, milord," she lied.

He departed, pausing outside to the lock the door.

CHAPTER 14

James accepted a cool tankard of ale to quench his thirst once he sat next to Red in the great hall. He gulped greedily, contemplating Elena's influence over him. There was so much more to her than he'd ever expected. Not only was she clever and beautiful, she had him questioning his life.

A servant approached.

"Eggs," James requested, displeased with his lingering lust. He preferred being in control.

"Tis the Lenten season, my lord. May I offer you some leeks poached in white wine?"

"Pork."

"All meat is forbidden until Easter Sunday. Almond soup? Bread?"

He grunted his approval and both items were placed on his trencher.

Red patted his shoulder and leaned close. "Edward is a woman." It was a statement, not a question.

James contemplated his friend's assessment, and after taking another long drink, he had no choice but to confess.

"Aye"

"*He* never pissed or bathed with the other lads."

James burst out laughing. He remembered eyeing her white arse in the woods. "It was better thinking her a lad. I only discovered the ruse after we returned to Nunnery."

Red studied him closely.

"At first, I wanted to punish, him-er-her," he admitted. "I felt betrayed. But, well—we came to an agreement."

"In your bed, I assume?"

Now it was his turn to scrutinize his friend. What could he say? That he was a fool in love? That would not do. Instead, he'd keep to the subject of training. "I agreed to continue to school her. But as a woman, she needs to be tamed like a spirited mare."

"And a fine ride she will be when you do."

James growled.

"Referring to horses," Red corrected.

Desiring a change in subject, James said, "About Nicholas—"

"Tis said he can fight equally well with both hands. Could pose some challenges."

"It makes him a more worthy opponent," James said, his jaw stiffening. "The man must die."

"Remember your training, James. Emotions are as hazardous as water. Keep yours hidden or you could drown."

James pounded a fist on the table. "I must avenge my father's death."

"We were once enemies. You lost against me because of your anger. I spared your life."

"I'm always grateful, but shortly after, I saved *you*, horse thief." James relaxed then. "If not for the Order, you might be an outlaw on the Spanish seas."

Red grunted, and they continued to discuss their strategy for the battle. After a couple hours, the hall grew quiet and

James yawned. He needed sleep. He bid his friend goodnight and made his way back to his chamber, careful not to disturb the servants sleeping on the floor. All he could think about was Elena waiting for him.

When he unlocked the door and entered his room, he noticed the fire had nearly gone out. She was scrunched into a tight ball on his bed. Immediately, he felt guilty for leaving her locked in. *Blasted woman!* She'd interrupted his simple life.

A female squire? What would his men say if they found out? He actually preferred *Edward*. But nothing about the girl in his bed reminded him of the boy.

She rolled over, and James sat on the edge of the bed admiring her. When he closed his fingers around her hand, his pulse quickened. He was hungry for her.

How would Elena respond if he woke her with a ravenous kiss? She'd ignited his passion when she offered herself to him after he'd rescued her from the forester's prison. Groaning, he let her hand go, then cupped her cheek, wrestling with his lust. The vows he'd taken forbid marriage, *not* sex.

Bedding willing women gave him release, but it was not the same with Elena. He wouldn't use her body or compromise her reputation. James cursed under his breath, his gaze sweeping over her body before he covered her with a fur. Even if the blanket were made of steel, it couldn't protect her if he followed through with what he wanted. He positioned himself on the far side of the mattress, trying to get comfortable, but tossed and turned.

Hours later, when sunlight filtered into his chamber, he moaned. Damn his feelings. He flipped over, facing the door, not expecting the vision that greeted him. Was he dreaming?

Elena was bathing and began stroking her breasts with a linen cloth. How he wished to trade places with it. Her nipples were pink and hard.

James groaned with pleasure, imagining what it would feel like to take her in his arms. After a frustrated breath, he closed his eyes, pretending to be asleep. Just as he began to relax . . .

"On your feet," she commanded. "Prepare to defend yourself."

His eyes flew open. She stood at the side of his bed, wearing nothing but a linen shirt, clutching his sword in both hands.

"I cannot get up." He was fully erect and didn't want her to see what affect her beauty had on him.

"Are you afraid?" she asked.

"More than you'll ever know," he muttered.

"James," someone called from the hallway. "It's time."

He caught Elena's attention and nodded toward the screen in the corner, trusting she'd understand. He didn't want to be caught like this.

"Enter," James called, just after she'd hidden herself.

Tristan walked in. "It's getting late, we must prepare for battle."

* * *

Elena had been grateful for Tristan's interruption that morn. As she worked in the stables, thinking about the encounter, she hadn't wanted to fight James. But the sword had been her only defense, her best chance at recovering her pride. And he'd been watching her bathe. She was thrilled and embarrassed. The brute feigned sleep, too afraid to admit how he truly felt about her.

Now as she worked in Dragon's stall, tightening the last of the armor under the horse's belly, she wondered if her time with James would end after the competition. Once his mother returned, no doubt the knights and squires would be reassigned. Would he still agree to keep her?

Elena had dreaded this day. Secretly, she'd hoped Sir Nicholas would've accepted the payment the duke had offered even though she understood James's desire to kill him. Honor hung in the balance. Something a bastard like Nicolas would never understand.

Dragon snorted, bringing her back to the task at hand. Getting him ready was going to require her full attention. Today she'd have to set aside her worries and help her knight win.

"You there, boy."

Elena wasn't expecting company. She turned. The man wore leather boots and an embroidered cloak, the collar decorated with precious stones. It took her a moment to realize he was the man from the prison. She never thought he'd make an appearance here.

"Can I help you, milord?" Would he recognize her in the squire's clothing?

"I'm looking for a lady who promised to be my escort today."

"Women do not frequent the stables."

He huffed, clearly frustrated. "I thought she'd be with Sir James's horse. Dragon, isn't it?"

"Yes, but why would a lady be here?"

"No one else could ride the beast from what I heard."

"I don't know who you are referring to, sir."

"Leave it to a stable boy to know nothing. I will find her myself."

Elena wiped her forehead with the back of her hand, thankful he didn't recognize her.

CHAPTER 15

elaying her entry to the tournament field for as long as she could, Elena finally left Dragon's stall with her head low as she walked to the new tiltyard contemplating the consequences of Sir Nicholas's arrival.

She had promised to be his escort and assumed he'd want to collect on what he called *favors*. But if he couldn't find the woman he'd met at the prison, then that part of the deal would be nullified. Nicholas had never been known to fulfil his promises. He deserved some of the same.

She scanned the stands. To the west, they were filled with knights, squires, and royal archers. The mayor, aldermen, lords and ladies, and the duke were seated on the opposite side. She relaxed a little when she didn't see him in the throng. But she wouldn't let her guard down.

"Good people," called the herald over the crowd. "Take your seats." He whirled his steed around with skill. "Get behind the barricades," he directed stragglers in the crowd. "Get back, unless you want God to take you before your time."

Next, a procession of officials poured into the field. First, the master-of-arms, followed by the junior officers. After much ceremony, the constable and head marshal took their respective seats. Then four mounted men-at-arms rode to each corner of the ring, joined by the marshals.

With everyone in place, a hush fell over the crowd. The master-at-arms held up his hand.

"A fight to the death" he announced. Then he turned to address the waiting judges. "Good gentlemen, please take your seats."

Elena secured her blue cap and scanned the grounds again.

Across the field, James appeared hungry for action, with his warhorse pawing the ground beneath him. Suited in full armour, his family crest emblazoned on his breastplate, her knight was an imposing figure on the competition field.

Although Isabel had offered to throw the rune stones to predict the outcome, Elena preferred to let fate play out. She was confident in James's abilities. Her knight was the most skilled of the order. And as she'd learned from his many awards, he had an impressive history of victory.

She looked to the other end of the list where Sir Nicolas sat tall in his saddle, his horse covered in protective ringmail.

Yet, no matter how many layers of armor he donned, she knew a coward and murderer hid beneath.

Red approached. "Are you ready?"

"I'm not afraid," she said.

Red stepped back, thoroughly assessing her. Honestly, she felt invincible. This wasn't James's battle alone. It was hers, too.

"I have a secret to share with you about James," he whispered. "I will wait to see if our friend survives the battle before I tell you."

She stared at him. He couldn't so easily tempt her. "He'll win," she said. "The angels will protect him."

Red chuckled. "Such faith for a whelp. Aye, the odds are in his favor, but we must do our part to support him."

She nodded. She'd do anything to assure her knight's victory.

"Ready your mounts," an official in the stands shouted.

James and Sir Nicolas responded immediately, urging their horses to their respective positions.

A trumpet sounded the official start. The white flag dropped and the crowd jumped to their feet.

Dragon broke away first, racing down the tilt at a hard gallop. The knights' lances collided, splintering into hundreds of pieces. Both riders jerked about, readying for another pass.

Elena was captivated by the scene. Both men had ridden with equal skill. But she wondered why James's direct hit to Nicolas's breastplate hadn't unseated him.

James snatched a new lance from her hands.

Again the flag dropped, and the horses thundered toward each other, dirt flying behind them.

James landed another brutal blow, Nicolas missing his mark. But neither fell.

Elena gritted her teeth when he returned to her for a fresh weapon and yanked it from her hands. Stymied by the results of her knight's lances, she wondered what more he could do to knock his opponent from the saddle?

Suddenly, Red rushed over to her as James was getting into position for the next pass.

"Check the swords and shields," he advised. "If the lances have been meddled with, the other weapons may have, too."

Together they made a cursory inspection. "I don't know," Elena said as she sorted through the weapons at the ready.

Red shook his head, clearly frustrated, but grabbed a shield and ran to the tilt, reaching the double palisade just as the warhorses surged forward.

Elena watched as both riders connected. James was unseated on impact, hitting the ground with a deafening thud. She struggled to stay put, her personal feelings nearly overriding her duty.

Let him get up on his own.

"Hold," shouted one of the officials.

Two marshals entered the field, each approaching the riders' horses.

Then the master-at-arms entered the ring. "The contest will now commence on foot," he announced. "We shall give each competitor time to prepare."

As she joined Red and James to walk the short distance to his pavilion tent, she shouted, "Devil's blood. You saw the lances snap like twigs."

Red nodded in agreement. "I'm certain the bastard tampered with them. But there's no time to challenge him."

"Am I working with two squabbling women or competent squires?" James asked. "Forget your suspicions. Give me your full attention."

Both in agreement, after making the required changes, Elena followed Red and James back to the tiltyard.

Now, instead of wearing heavy armor, both knights donned simple chainmail. James chose an open helmet. Nicolas wore a full helm, his face shielded from view.

The knights met in the middle of the field, both surrendering their swords to the marshal for quick inspection.

The official nodded in approval. "Begin."

Neither man hesitated, charging with their longswords raised high.

James was an elite swordsman. He swore battles were won this way, not by jousting. And as long as his weapon was sound, Elena was certain he'd defeat Nicolas. She edged closer to Red. "Should I inspect the other swords and shields more closely?"

"We have no time for that. Ask Tristan for his weapons instead."

Although she didn't wan to miss a moment's of the sword fight, she forced herself to look away and headed in Tristan's direction.

But James's curses forced her to turn abruptly.

"Devil's work," he exclaimed. His blade had separated from its handle. Tossing that aside, he immediately grabbed his battle axe from his holster.

Elena gasped. Red's suspicions were correct. She turned, ready to rushed to Tristan. But he had already joined her. "Here, take my sword and shield."

She wasn't far from the fighting, but Elena returned to the field just as James charged Sir Nicolas. Her knight looked like a mythic warrior. A chill went up her spine.

Nicholas spun out of the way and James lost his balance, falling to his knees.

Elena feared the worst, and cried out.

"It's your time to die," Sir Nicholas declared, swinging his weapon, striking James in the back.

Elena couldn't believe what she was seeing. The crowd remained silent as James fell face first into the dirt.

CHAPTER 16

*E*lena was horrified. Stabbed in the back again? Could the fates be so cruel?

The dark knight raised his bloody sword. Was Sir Nicholas laughing?

Red, Tristan, and a few others rushed to James. She hesitated to join them. What good could she do pining away by his side?

Unmoving and silent, once again she had to face the possibility that her beloved knight might be dead. If not, he'd likely perish soon. Would his enemy let him bleed out or finish him off? She wouldn't wait.

Driven by raw emotions, she ignored her lack of protective armor, as well as Red's warnings to stay away, and instead, raced across the field clutching Tristan's weapon. She had nothing left to live for. The bastard needed to pay for what he'd done to James and his family.

When she struck the first blow, she felt triumphant, slamming Sir Nicholas in the back of the helmet so hard he stumbled forward. She followed-through again, hacking a notch out of the knight's right shoulder plate. The clanging of steel and the cheers of the crowd reminded Elena this was no game.

Fully expecting retaliation, she was thankful her attack had rattled him. Even though Sir Nicholas was a brute, he spun around aimlessly chopping his sword through the air.

Before she had a chance to thank her patron saint, the combatant regained his wits and came charging towards her in a sudden bull rush.

She drew in a deep breath, then ducked under his arm, successfully avoiding his assault.

The knight swore loudly, reeling around, staring at her. Again he charged, choosing to use raw strength over skill, and just as he was upon her, Elena stuck her boot out and tripped him. Then she thrust her sword into his mail, above the elbow.

The crowd screamed.

He doubled over, blood wet the crook of his arm, seeping out the top of his gauntlet, but the injury didn't stop him. Nicolas swung again and again with fury, but with little accuracy. Even when he switched hands, each thrust was slower than the last.

Finally, it became clear that her opponent didn't possess the endurance to defeat her. She took advantage of his weakness, sprinting to the other side of the circle, preparing for his next advance, a tactic she'd learned from James. If the enemy was bigger and stronger, let him wear himself out.

Elena's resolve was unwavering. She blocked out Red's voice, the crowd, marshals, and even James's lifeless body. Her fears were secondary; vengeance her only companion.

And perhaps God's will.

She prayed, keeping her eyes fixed on Nicholas. "Lord, please keep me from harm and allow me to perform beyond my expectations."

Glancing heavenward as if to seal her prayer, she noticed

the sky had turned dark and menacing. But an ear-piercing scream from Sir Nicholas broke her concentration. A clap of thunder burst in the air, followed by a flash of lightning. The heavens opened up, rain began to pound the earth.

Unfortunately the storm didn't hinder her enemy; his armor shielded him from the rain. He pressed forward, lashing out.

She readied herself, willing to accept her fate. Suddenly the temperature dropped, and the rain turned to sleet. Elena shivered, but didn't give up. The ice pelted her body, but didn't hurt. Were the angels beside her?

But Sir Nicholas . . . The ice bombarded his injured body. It sounded like a war hammer hitting a rock. He dropped his sword and loosened his chin strap, then stumbled around like a drunkard.

"Praise the Almighty," she cried. The Lord's own hands were working a miracle, and she'd take full advantage.

She gritted her teeth and readied her sword, waiting for him to remove his helmet. She'd slice through his skull like a summer melon. When he did, she struck with all her might, the borrowed longsword nearly severing his bloody head.

Cheers sounded all around her. Where had she gotten the strength to do this? But now the weapon weighed heavy in her hands, so she dropped it, falling to her knees. Would her soul be spared the fires in Hades?

"Edward . . . Edward . . . Edward . . ." the crowd chanted. Her gaze drifted from her fallen enemy to the joyous spectators. Numb with sorrow, she'd never be able to celebrate the taking of a life, even if God sanctioned the death himself.

She heard a clamor from behind.

"He lives."

Had Sir Nicholas cheated death again? She blinked rapidly, turning on her knees. No, Nicholas was dead. But *James* lived.

Without thought, she climbed to her feet, then ran to James's side, throwing herself on top of him. She kissed him, unafraid of what anyone would think or say. And to her shock and surprise, her knight returned her fevered kisses with equal passion, framing her face with both hands.

With a deep laugh he yanked her cap off, stroking her hair. His large hands roved over her shoulders and down her back. *Alive!* She had risked her life not to save him, but avenge him. God had intervened, giving her a second chance with James. Isabel would say it was fate.

As quickly as her body heated laying on top of the man she loved, someone dumped cold water over them, a rude reminder of where they were. On the tournament field.

"God's blood." James released her, his thunderous outburst prompting Red's laughter.

"Men, 'tis not what you think." James's words were muffled when her hungry lips sought his out again. "Edward is Elena. A woman, not a man," he tried to explain.

More ribald comments followed.

Tristan came to stand over them. "The chain mail and the heavy metal backplate protected you from what Nicholas thought was your end."

James nodded. "And he must have slipped when he charged for the force was not that mighty. Or I may not be talking with you now," he admitted.

Shaking his head in apparent disbelief Tristan chuckled. "At first I thought James befuddled by the fall, striking his head too hard on the ground," he joked. "But I couldn't come up with an excuse for Edward's behavior."

Snorting as he gently pushed her off him and managing to sit up, James scanned the area.

Elena followed his gaze and quickly became aware of a growing audience of curious villagers and nobles. She couldn't blame them. She was dressed like a squire and her magnificent knight had made no attempt to hide his feelings for her.

"Elena," James said, "ever since we left Warwickshire, you have insisted you could fight. And you have proven that to me today. Let us celebrate. Red, assist Lady Elena."

Red plucked her up, setting her on her feet next to the surgeon who was pulling items out of his satchel.

James groaned as he staggered to his feet and she now could asses his back armor. The gash was deep where Nicolas had struck.

"Stay still, Sir James," the healer insisted.

He grunted. "I've been on my arse long enough," he said. "There's time to mend once we're out of public view. Let me enjoy this moment with Elena." He smiled at her, pain apparent on his handsome face.

"The secret is out, Elena," Red whispered after he pulled her aside.

Elena gazed at him, fully aware of what risks she'd taken protecting James. Inquiries would follow. She'd broken a dozen sacred laws, lied about her identity, dressed as a boy in a room full of men without a chaperone, and slept in James's bed.

"I have no defense," she admitted. "Except love."

And she'd do it again if it meant sparing the life of the man she cared for.

"Not that secret," Red clarified. "But the one I promised to share with you after the joust. James loves you."

She gasped, her legs suddenly weak. With Red holding her elbow, he guided her to the center of the arena to join the head marshal. She had spent weeks disguised and had enjoyed certain liberties. That was about to change.

"Good people, tarry here for a moment longer," the master-at-arms requested. "Sir James wishes to address you."

Assisted by the surgeon, James stood in front of the spectators and raised his hands. "Before you is my squire. Not Edward, but the Lady Elena of Warwickshire. This woman saved my life. Pay homage to her."

Again the crowd cheered.

She was half way into a bow, when she changed her mind and curtsied. Even though she could fight like a man, it was time to start acting like a lady again.

James let out a grunt that turned into a groan, while clutching his side. He gave her a sideways glance. He was doing his best to hide the pain. She was thrilled that he'd given her a proper introduction. Yes, there would be whispers and questions, but she couldn't think of a better time to shed her boy's clothes.

The joy was short-lived. Just as she was turning to follow the master-at-arms, she felt a jolt to her shoulder. Myrddin, her precious bird, had returned. And then it occurred to her. *The nobleman must know who I am and how to find me.*

CHAPTER 17

"*E*lena Louise Catherine," Isabel shouted, pacing restlessly in the guest quarters. Her cousin shook her head in disgust "You could have been killed. Then what?"

"*You* would've buried me," Elena said soberly, thankful that she had survived the melee. "At that moment, when I thought James was gone, I didn't want to live any longer."

Isabel let out a long, loud sigh, her expression changing from concern to understanding. "You are past the point of no return."

Elena nodded.

Sitting cross-legged on the edge of the bed, Elena was happy that the duke had insisted she have a room in the women's quarters after the fight. Of course it had been irresponsible of her to confront Sir Nicholas. But she didn't regret it. God had a hand in her success.

"Come now, the secret's out." Isabel handed her a dress. "What are you going to do about it?"

"This." Elena removed her chemise, then tugged the gown over her head, pushing her arms through the long, flared sleeves. Made of the softest blue velvet, and trimmed in bands of gold, it hugged her curves perfectly. She crossed the room and admired herself in the polished glass.

Finally, she looked like a woman again, well almost. She groaned. Her hair was gaining length again and pooled in curls at her shoulders, but there was nothing she could do about it. She tucked a loose strand behind her ear, then sighed. "Isabel…"

"Let me help," her cousin offered.

After fishing a few hairpins out of her pocket, Isabel began twisting sections of Elena's hair, securing it on top of her head, loose curls framing her face. Next she fashioned a wreath of blue irises taken from a vase on the wardrobe. With the flowers crowning her head, Elena felt like a queen.

Stepping back, Isabel studied her work. "Oh, my, if James wasn't in love with you already . . ."

Elena chuckled. "On Red's word. More likely there's a wager between them. I've yet to see the proof, but James won't recognize me because I'll be wearing this." She snatched her last accessory off the table, putting it on. She spun around, staring in the mirror. The intricate, gold-embossed mask concealed her identity.

Isabel walked behind her. "Aren't you finished with disguises, Elena?"

She rolled her eyes. "Remember, it's Hocktide, everyone in the great hall will be wearing one."

Isabel clucked her tongue. "Be careful, James is drunk. I met him in the corridor on my way here with your gown. I'd stay away from him if I were you."

"Too much celebrating over Sir Nicholas's death?"

Isabel shook a warning finger. "Men can't be trusted when they are intoxicated. Don't be naïve."

"I merely want to have a look. I'll stay out of his way," she promised, anxious to get to the victory celebration.

After thanking Isabel, Elena made her way to the great

hall. Although Lady Victoria's welcome dinner would not be until tomorrow, the room was full of celebrants. In accordance with the traditions of Hocktide, the ladies were the suitors, which in her mind, would work to her advantage. Even masked, Elena spotted James easily, his hair unmistakable. Sitting on the steps at the north end of the hall alone, he appeared bored with the entire affair.

She edged closer with scandalous intent. "Celebrating, milord?"

"Aren't we all?" he asked, his words a bit slurred.

She nodded in agreement. "Sir Nicholas is dead."

"I'll drink to that." He downed the rest of his wine, staring at her.

"Some company, milord?"

James removed his mask, his heated gaze sweeping over her. "You appear in need of an escort," he said, standing.

She smiled. "Isn't the purpose of the night for all ladies to have the right to choose whose company they keep?" The thought of going anywhere with him alone excited her.

He offered his hand, and she took it without hesitation. "To my chambers?" he offered. "I promise no one will disturb us there."

"But who would keep me safe from you?"

He tossed his head back, roaring with laughter. "Well, my lady, that's a question I cannot answer. Join me and we may find out."

Elena nodded and he guided her under the archway and up the stairs to his solar, certain he didn't know who she was. Which suggested Red's words were empty. If James loved her, why would he take another woman to his chamber? Even drunk, it wasn't an excuse in her mind. But she was willing to find out before she confronted him.

Once inside, Elena approached the four-poster bed

swathed with red curtains. The space was warmed by a pleasant fire.

She watched as he slid the bolt in place. The Hocktide had given her the opportunity she desperately needed to get James alone. He'd already told her he wouldn't compromise her. With Nicholas dead, and his mother due home in the morning, this night might be her only chance to prove how she felt.

James began unbuttoning his linen shirt as he came at her. When he reached her, he dropped the garment on the floor. Within seconds he was completely naked, unashamed and ready for whatever she offered. The thought made her throat go dry as she stared at him, admiring his splendid body.

He beckoned with a wicked grin and extended his arms. "Will you take me prisoner for Hocktide?"

"Consider yourself captured," she said, grasping his wrists.

"Are you giving yourself to me?"

She nodded, unable to speak.

"Don't be afraid, milady. Though I'll warn you, I don't have much patience when I see something I want. Turn around."

She hesitated, caught between love and tradition. If she offered herself to him and they were found out . . .

"Don't think about it too long my sweet." He cupped her cheek. "I want you out of that damn dress." He gently spun her around.

With his help, she stripped it off. When she turned to face him again, she covered her breasts, gazing up at him.

"It's all right, love, I won't bite." He chuckled as he tugged her to his chest, the warmth of his skin on hers excited her.

His hands moved up her ribs, exploring freely, eliciting pleasurable sensations all over her body. When his thumbs slid over her hard nipples, she groaned, her eyes widening in confusion. After just a few caresses, she ached for him. How could that be?

"Close your eyes," he said softly, nipping her earlobe. Elena did as he asked, her heart pounding.

James nipped her ear again. "Let me show you how much I desire you." He released her long enough for her to miss the warmth of his body. But before she could complain, a different kind of heat rose between them. He rolled his hips, pressing his shaft against her belly. Her eyes popped open. Did he recognize her even with the mask still on?

James swept her up, carrying her to the edge of the bed. After he set her down, he crawled beside her, feathering kisses down her neck, caressing her breasts. His hot breath tickled her skin. Then he captured a nipple between his teeth, his fingers working the other, teasing and provoking feelings she'd never felt before. He licked his way up her center, finding her hungry mouth again.

The first kiss was slow and delicious. He tasted like wine. Their tongues danced together, James slowly summoning all her hidden passion. As his tongue slid deeper, she let out a cry. He stopped, his eyes flickering with desire.

* * *

JAMES BLOOD RACED through his body like a stampede of wild horses. He was losing control. At first, the flirting seemed innocent enough, he thought even to teach her a lesson. The mask, a childish disguise, didn't hide the woman he'd come to know. Her body, her scent, her voice, were all familiar now. Even sotted, he was no idiot.

With a naked Elena in his bed, he faced a sobering reality. There was no stopping his heart now. He'd grown to care about her, maybe too much.

"My prisoner," she whispered.

"You cannot take a willing man captive. Be kind with your torture, milady."

He came undone when she writhed against him. Did she know what she was doing to him?

James cupped her head in his hands and gently pulled her face towards his, crushing his mouth to hers. He too could play the same game. While he devoured her lips, he slid his fingers down her back, sampling her soft flesh. But what he preferred most, was her tiny arse, and he cupped it with both hands and rolled her onto her back. Elena whimpered, feeding his need even more.

Trailing his lips over the tops of each breast, he then flicked his tongue around her nipples, eliciting groans of pleasure.

"Take me," she begged breathlessly, her hands running over his body, then grasping and tugging his hair wildly. "You're my first ."

His heart skipped a beat. "First?"

"Yes." She stared up at him.

Her claim snapped him back to reality. Making love to an experienced woman was one thing, deflowering a maiden for the sake of pleasure, another. "We must end this," he said sternly. He'd rather have his throat slit by Sir Nicholas than take her virginity.

"I'm quite drunk and need my rest. You should go."

"Go?"

"Yes," he snapped. He didn't know what else to do.

She dressed silently, refusing to meet his gaze again. As she closed the door, James regretted his refusal, but knew it was better for both of them. He'd sate his lust himself.

here was Tristan and his mother? James paced as he kept watch. His captain had left for Cadbury Castle in the morning, along with the tournament marshals, and the head of Sir Nicholas to prove the outcome of the tournament. They should have been back by now.

At the duke's insistence, the entire court of Nunnery waited inside the great hall to receive the duchess. Anxious to greet her, James, Richard, and Elena waited at the entrance together.

Elena kept him reasonably distracted. Blasted woman. He couldn't keep his eyes off her, nor could anyone else. Dressed in a flattering red gown, with a wreath of white roses atop her head, no one would mistake her for a boy anymore. And after last night, the memories of her natural beauty and willingness to share his bed, haunted him. Curse God for the complications that plagued his life. How could he honor his oaths and not forsake her at the same time. He hoped maybe a word with his mother would help.

After waiting about another hour, he was ready to saddle

Dragon and set out to find his mother on his own, when Tristan finally entered the great hall with a retinue.

As they approached, James searched for his precious mother. She wasn't amongst them and his anger stirred.

Sir Richard stepped forward and spoke briefly with Tristan, then he faced James. "The terms have changed," he announced with an emotionless expression.

The crowd gasped.

"Changed?" James repeated. "How?"

"I'm afraid the *real* Duke of Dunster is very much alive," Richard added.

"We meet again," Sir Nicholas said defiantly, revealing himself from behind the tournament marshals.

"You are not welcome here." James moved forward, now realizing the wrong man had died.

"Hear him out," Richard urged.

James fought to contain his anger. "There is nothing this man can say that would convince me that he shouldn't be dead," he claimed as if he had the king's permission to make it so. Then he walked to within inches of the man's face, ready to finish the bastard off.

Sir Nicholas laughed.

James raised his fisted hand, but his stepfather caught it midair. "No," he insisted. "He has your mother."

"Nay, I won't listen. This man deserves a quick death. With God's help, I'll finish it now." He jerked his hand free, then grabbed Nicholas's throat. Strangling the devil with his bare hands would be more satisfying than striking a death-blow with a sword.

But his efforts were interrupted when Red gripped his shoulders from behind. "James, remember the Garter oath."

He exhaled in frustration and let go of Nicolas. Nothing had ever tempted him to kill without a second thought.

Nicholas coughed violently. "You have something that

belongs to me." He walked over to Elena, who stood staring at the earl as if she'd seen a ghost. He grabbed one of her hands.

James lurched forward, claiming the other. "She is mine. Let her go." He tightened his hold on her hand.

"Your squire is coming with me." Nicholas tugged her arm.

The muscles in James's shoulders tensed. "I won't say it again, she's mine. You have no right to claim her."

"You're wrong. Elena is the new wager," Nicolas argued. But then the nave stepped back and released her hand. "No, I shall let you choose after all . . ." Laughing wickedly, the earl assumed a cocky stance, stroking his chin, venomous eyes glaring. "Your mother or your squire?"

To hell with the method, any means of killing the devil would be satisfying. He too released Elena, then stalked forward, shoving Nicolas back. "Coward."

The crowd gasped. Elena ran for cover while Red and Tristan rushed forward, both jerking longswords from their hilts.

"Enough!" Red called.

Nicholas laughed mockingly. "Come now, you wouldn't kill an unarmed man. The very vows you believe make you a formidable knight, actually make you weak."

"The law affords me the right to slit your throat." James stalked closer again, eyes focused on Nicolas.

"I refuse to be bullied." Nicholas turned to the duke. "If I knew how uncivilized your men were, I'd have sent a messenger instead."

"That was your first mistake," the duke said. "The second was taking my wife prisoner." Now the duke drew his weapon. "I have just as much reason to kill you."

"I'm the king's cousin." He glanced at them. "Commit treason? I dare you."

When James looked sideways at the duke, his stepfather gave him a firm nod.

Nicholas suddenly retreated. "I refuse to fight," he shouted.

James punched Nicolas in the jaw, knocking the man off his feet. Then he stared at his motionless form, grinning when the crowd cheered.

"Can I count on you to return this vermin to where he came from?" James asked Red.

He nodded.

"I will not accept this man's terms. That's a consequence I cannot live with."

Red patted him on the back. "I know we'll come up with a plan."

James nodded, then glanced around the hall. "Where's Elena?"

"The duke had Tristan escort her to her room."

"To keep her in, or me out?" James asked.

Red laughed. "Come, James, help me haul this piece of shite outside."

CHAPTER 19

*E*lena was leaving. Not to escape to Warwickshire, but to seek restitution from Sir Nicolas. The man had deceived her and was trying to manipulate James now. She couldn't let that happen. Although James didn't know the half of it, she wouldn't make him choose between her and his beloved mother.

Even after feeling the sting of James rejection the other night, and the fact that he'd agreed to sleep with another woman, even though it had been her, Elena still wanted to support the man she loved. Isabel helped her escape the castle by luring the guard away from her door.

Dressed in her squire clothes, she made it to the lower bailey. The flickering torchlight in the stables helped her find her way to Dragon's stall, knowing he'd be the best horse for the task ahead.

No one noticed her ride away from the castle.

* * *

VICTORIA HEAVED A WEARY SIGH. She'd just finished adding another mark to the wall with a stone, the only way she could keep track of how many days she'd been held against her will. Thirty-four to be exact.

Suddenly a commotion broke out in the hall.

"Come now, quit squirming. You were caught sneaking into the castle. You'll have to be punished," a guard spoke harshly.

Another prisoner?

"Once Sir Nicolas returns, you can plead your case to him," he added. "Until then . . ."

A scruffy-looking lad was shoved into her cell. The guard slammed the door and the boy fell to his knees, hanging his head. Certain he didn't see her in the shadows, Victoria broke the silence. "What have you done to deserve the wrath of Sir Nicholas?"

The boy jumped, but didn't answer.

"Come, do not fear me," she spoke softly as she approached. "I too am a captive here." She touched his shoulder.

"I am ashamed to tell you my story, milady," he muttered. "I'd rather die."

"Nothing is worth dying for except your country and honor," she countered. "'Tis what my son, a Knight of the Garter, always says."

"I guess that's true, but I gave my word and now I want to take it back. I'm ashamed," the lad muttered.

"I've no fate worse than yours. We can share our stories." She eyed the boy. "I'll go first."

Victoria began to pace the small cell, certain revealing her past would absolve her of any sin. *And if the bastard kills me,* she thought, *someone must know the truth.*

"The lord who commands this castle was once my husband," she started. "He's holding me here in hopes he can kill my son in exchange for my freedom. But I fear he'll take my life, too."

"Sir Nicholas was once your husband?" the boy asked, staring at her.

"Aye, Nicholas, Earl of Dunster. I will not call him sir or lord, but that is his title. He tried to kill my son once before. When James was only a lad. That was the night he murdered my first husband, Sir Rafe de Saxton, then turned on the boy. He believed James to be Rafe's son."

The boy's expression turned sympathetic, as if he somehow felt her pain.

"A few years later, Nicholas came back into my life. He threatened me, told me I would lose everything I owned if I didn't marry him. He had the power to ruin me. A man's word is always accepted over a woman's. So I embraced this fate, marrying him in name only, just after James left for the order." She took a deep breath. "The saddest part? James is really Nicholas's son. That devil raped me when I was fifteen, before I married Rafe. He doesn't know James is his flesh and blood."

There was more to the dark tale. Rafe and Nicholas had served as knights together. But that was another story.

"I cannot believe Nicolas and James aren't aware of their relation."

She shook her head. "Nicholas only cares about power. He'll do anything to advance himself, even commit murder."

"How is it that you're married to the duke then?"

"In exchange for my family's land in Scotland, Nicholas was banished from Somerset. The church annulled my marriage for the right price. Praise the Lord he wasn't there to contest it. But because he is of the new king's blood, Nicholas has come back to claim all I own."

"If he wants you dead, why hasn't he murdered you already?"

The little urchin has a point. Why hasn't he? "Now promise me," she pleaded. "If Nicholas kills me, you'll find James and tell him everything I've shared."

The lad gave her a sideways glace and nodded.

"Good. Now your turn."

He coughed. "I'm not who I seem, my lady." The boy removed his cap. "Like you, I've been concealing secrets of my own."

Victoria nodded.

"I know your son. He was fostered every summer in Warwickshire," the boy said.

Victoria smiled. "Aye, with my Uncle John."

The boy stood, then walked toward her, smiling for the first time. "His property bordered my father's lands. There was little to do, and somehow James and I became friends."

She stared at the lad. The walk. The face. Something was wrong. "You're not a boy."

The lad shook his head.

"Elena?" Victoria asked.

"Indeed, my lady."

"Come here, dear."

Victoria remembered Elena. A true beauty even at a young age. How had she crossed Nicholas? "Elena, why are you in disguise?"

"I'm in love with James," she confessed. "I lied to be close to him. I dressed as a boy to be his squire."

"You love my son? Weren't you promised to another?"

"I was once betrothed to a boy named Thomas, but it was not a love match. I refused to spend any time with him and sought solace in the woods. One day I fell from a tree. If it weren't for your son's help, I could have died."

"My son has always been a brave man. Did you fall in love because he saved you?"

"No," Elena assured her. "James and I met well before the

fall. He taught me how to fight and made me laugh. Then, we shared an unbreakable bond."

"You defied your father's wishes to spend time with my son?" Victoria asked.

Elena nodded. "James promised to make me his bride one day, after he became a great knight."

"James would never break a promise."

"I believe you. But recently told me that he made another pledge. Never to marry. In doing so, he could dedicate his life to the Order."

"Aye," she said. "I asked him never to marry, too. I have my reasons." Victoria sighed, fate had a cruel way of playing tricks on people. This poor girl loved her son. "Why are you here, Elena?"

"To rescue you."

Victoria couldn't help but laugh.

CHAPTER 20

Stealing past the guard proved easier than Victoria imagined. She'd been able to reach through the bars and dispense the herbs in the soldier's tankard after he'd left his post to get their bread rationing. He downed the ale as soon as he returned.

Before she could count to twenty, the man slumped over. She was able to reach his keys and release them. Then she relocked the door and returned them to the guard's belt. With any luck, they wouldn't be found missing until they were safely back behind the walls of Nunnery.

Outside the cell, Victoria put her finger to her lips and waved Elena over. "Follow close. Remember, I know the castle."

As she led Elena out of the prison tower and into the keep, her heart beat wildly at every turn. Each shadow a threat. But her confidence returned when they finally reached the kitchen and she spotted Cook.

"There's Esmeralda," she whispered, pushing Elena toward the entrance.

No doubt the large woman heard them coming when she

spun around. Her mouth dropped open when she spied the two of them.

"Lady Victoria?" The servant's face softened. "Am I seeing a ghost?" The cook pinched her before she answered.

"Ouch," Victoria cried.

"You scared me to death," chastised the large woman. "Tis you, my lady, looking so frail. I'm the only one here." The cook embraced her.

"Oh, Esmeralda. Let me go, dear. I need your help," Victoria pleaded.

"The only way I can help is if I feed you first. No arguing," the servant insisted, walking to the stove. "You look like you haven't eaten in days."

"Thirty-four days of only stale bread and water, that's how long the bastard kept me in the dungeon." Victoria sighed, claiming a stool by the fire.

"What about this waif here? Are you together?"

"This is Elena, a friend of my son," she explained, licking her lips. The aroma of fresh bread reminded her how hungry she was.

"A girl? Under those britches?" Esmeralda walked to Elena and gave her a thorough examination and even pulled off her cap, which Elena grabbed and set on the table.

"A tale too long to share," Victoria commented. "Please, Esmeralda, pack some food for us. We can't stay." She didn't mean for her voice to sound so desperate or shrill, but she was anxious to leave. If Nicholas found them, he wouldn't hesitate to kill them.

Esmeralda began scooping up items and shoveling them into a large tablecloth. Minutes later, she had everything tied in a bundle.

"Mi lady, you must leave so soon?" the cook asked when she hugged Victoria.

"Upon my return, I'll dine on one of your famous peacock

stews." Victoria pried herself free of Esmeralda's tight grasp and snatched the food bundle off the table.

Then, as silently as possible, Victoria and Elena slipped into the shadows of the lower bailey.

* * *

CADBURY CASTLE STOOD atop the heavily wooded hilltop just a short distance from where James and his men rested their horses.

Fifteen years. Memories of his father's fatal sword fight stung now like a cut from a fresh blade.

Elena had to be somewhere close. Either in the nearby woods or inside the fortress. She was that naïve and bold. Somehow, she'd gotten past the night guard. Blasted woman! No doubt she'd left Nunnery with the intention of doing the choosing for him. No matter her shortcomings, he loved her and the Devil be damned, he'd find her.

With his knowledge of the fortress, he was confident they could get inside. An ancient tunnel dug deep below the hills would grant access to the dungeons. He just had to remember where it was.

Leading his men toward the hills jogged James's memory. They found the entrance to the tunnels without much trouble. Overgrown with weeds and brambles, his men hacked away at the stubborn branches until they uncovered a long forgotten wood door.

Once the lock was pried off, James struck his flint and a flame blazed bright, lighting the torch Red had found inside the entrance.

Knowing which route to take, James lead the way. But it wasn't long before they reached the end of that passage and another rotted doorway stood in their way.

He drove his shoulder against the barrier, but it didn't budge. "Lend a hand," James called. "I'll need the lot of you."

With a united effort, the rusty hinges finally gave way. They crashed through the doorway, landing on the flagstones inside the castle tower. James smiled, pleased with their progress so far.

He brushed dirt and debris from his hands and face, then turned to his men. "Red and I must go the rest of the way alone. Retrace your steps and hide yourselves just outside the entrance. If we're successful, I'll use the wolf call once we're outside the gates again. If dawn arrives first, ride hard to Nunnery for reinforcements."

With Red by his side, they searched cell after empty cell. But found nothing. Frustrated, James raised his gaze and silently prayed for God's assistance.

After they returned to the main corridor, they chose another off shoot and headed that direction. This time, a rotting stench stopped them.

James squinted, staring straight ahead, trying to make out what he saw in the distance. *Is that a guard?*

James signaled Red to follow. Foot by foot, they approached silently. At first glance, the solider appeared to be asleep at his table, but they'd take no chances.

Red struck the back of the guard's head with the handle of his dagger. After the sentry fell from his chair, James snatched the keys from his belt.

James unlocked the gate, then cautiously stepped inside the cavernous cell. It was empty like all the others, full of old armor, but no prisoners. Where was his mother? No one guarded an empty cell.

"Nothing here. Let's try the kitchen," James suggested. "There's always a servant at the hearth."

"James, the kitchen is this way. I can smell it," Red suggested.

"Over this stench? Nay," he chuckled, "it's this way." He pointed in the right direction, thankful he'd grown up here.

Minutes later, they entered the kitchen, startling the cook.

"What the devil?" The puffy-faced woman narrowed her gaze, silently challenging them. "The meal is over, get out."

"Is that any way to welcome weary knights?" James asked. "Don't you remember me, Esmeralda?"

She stared at him for a long moment, her gaze raking him head to toe. "James?" she whispered as if she didn't want Nicholas to hear. "My babe, James?" She rushed to embrace him.

"Yes, dear cook. I promised I would one day return to be your knight." He hugged her, happy to see her again.

She stepped back, smiling. "Praise God you're well. Who is with you?"

"My fellow knight, Sir Red. Mind this woman, friend," he warned, looking at Red. "I learned the hard way as a boy. Finding my arse red with swats from her wooden spoons."

"A pleasure to meet you." Red bowed. "Anyone brave enough to whip my friend, has my respect." He smiled.

Esmeralda blushed, clapping her hands together. "Are you here to see your mother?"

James wished there was more time to visit. He'd missed the cook and some of the other servants who had treated him well as a boy. "Was she here?" His heart soared.

"Yes, minutes ago. She's fleeing with another girl dressed as a lad. Both are trying to escape Nicolas."

"They were together?"

"Yes," the cook answered. "Look on the table, there's the lad's cap."

James stared at the familiar hat, the one Elena always wore.

"James," Red called. "Are you all right?"

James nodded.

"You must go," Esmeralda urged. "Once Nicholas discovers they are missing, he won't stop until they're dead."

CHAPTER 21

Nicholas was restless, fear of being murdered in his bed kept him up most nights. His selfish and brutal rules made him a prime target of people who despised him. One thing that alleviated the stress was cracking a whip against the back of a prisoner, especially one with virgin skin. And from what he recalled, there was another prisoner awaiting questioning in the tower.

His father taught him at an early age what true physical punishment meant. But the emotional scars he carried surpassed the physical pain he'd suffered. As the third son of an earl, he'd had little hope for power until he met Victoria.

At first, he'd envied her family's wealth, their land and titles, but he'd quickly fallen hopelessly in love with her. Over time, he slowly opened up to her, expecting her to understand his pain. Why hadn't she loved him back?

It didn't matter now. To hell with her.

Snatching a whip from the hook near his bed, he decided she wouldn't be spared his heavy hand. He walked to the connecting door.

"Rudolf," he called. "It's time to visit the prisoners. Now!"

His servant immediately rolled off his bed and grabbed a lit torch from the wall.

It wasn't long before they arrived at Victoria's cell, but the guard was lying on the floor and the keys where in the cell door.

Nicholas examined the guard closely.

"It appears our friend has been the victim of some violence. And that bitch will pay with her life." He cracked the whip against the stone wall, dust spitting everywhere.

"We must find them. Now!"

* * *

Elena slipped through the back entrance of Cadbury Castle's stables following Victoria. Fortunately, the guard was asleep. They ducked low, creeping around him, then Elena took the lead.

"Here he is," she whispered when they arrived at the last stall. "Isn't he beautiful?"

"Dragon? This is your plan? Only my son can ride this beast," Victoria hissed. "We must take another."

"My lady, I rode him here. He's as much my horse as James's. He *is* our only escape."

"Are you certain he won't buck me off?" Victoria asked, eyeing the horse nervously. She gestured to the other stalls. "There are other mounts I could ride."

"We must ride Dragon," Elena insisted.

"There is no other option?"

"Nay," she whispered. Why wouldn't she trust her judgment? "With his speed and endurance, we'll get away. And if we share the same mount, there's no danger of us getting separated."

Victoria nodded, then swung herself into the saddle like a seasoned rider.

Elena climbed behind her, praying for good luck. "Come boy," she urged. "Dragon, take us home."

* * *

JAMES AND RED watched as Nicholas rode across the bailey to join a group of mounted soldiers at the front gate. They were close enough to hear his orders.

"Two prisoners have escaped. The Duchess of Somerset and a nameless vagrant." Nicholas pointed his longsword at the large group. "No one leaves this castle. My man-at-arms will command the search here and I'll lead another party into the countryside. If you find them," he shouted, "drag them back in bloody chains."

James cursed. The women were free, but had they escaped? Motioning Red to follow him, they walked quickly to the stables.

After searching every stall and not finding Dragon, James heaved a sigh of relief. "It appears my mother and Elena are gone. But they aren't out of danger yet."

Red nodded. "Elena is a clever girl, she'll safeguard your mother. She's risking her life for you again."

James squeezed his friend's shoulder. "I've turned her into a knight. But is she Garter-worthy?"

"No woman is Garter-worthy, but she's proved worthy of something else. Something I'm sure she values above all things."

James cocked his head, afraid to hear the answer.

"Your heart."

"Impossible."

Red scoffed. "Don't live in denial, friend. The king has the power to absolve your vow, the right to grant you the freedom to marry."

"What makes you think that's what I want?"

Red shook his head. "You'd have to be a blind bastard not to see it."

CHAPTER 22

They had just reached the edge of Sedgemoor, the halfway point between Cadbury and Nunnery castles. And although Elena preferred to avoid the town completely, it would cost precious time to go around it. A clap of thunder made her nervous, the conditions were now dangerous.

"Victoria, we need shelter," she called over her shoulder. "Dragon will get skittish in this weather."

Victoria squeezed her tightly. "You promised we could ride this horse without getting bucked."

"He doesn't like thunder and lightning."

There were only a few hiding places to consider. Riding on the edge of town, Elena scanned the buildings.

"There." She pointed to a steeple just ahead. "We'll make our way to the abbey."

She circled the belfry on the other side of the cemetery and spotted an old barn. *That's the place.* Thankfully, she urged Dragon inside just as heavy rain began to fall. She helped Victoria dismount, then secured Dragon, happy they were safe and anxious to find the vicar.

"Ready?" Elena asked.

When Victoria nodded, the two dashed outside and across the cemetery. She followed Victoria up the ancient steps and into the church.

Pushing the heavy wooden door shut behind them, Elena spun around to find the vicar scurrying across the sanctuary to greet them.

"Come in," he offered. "Look at you. Both drenched." He grabbed linens off a table. "Take these."

Elena was thankful for the kind welcome. She shivered as she wiped herself off.

"What's brought you here on a night like this?" the priest asked.

She'd be direct. They desperately needed his help. "We're fugitives, Father," she confessed. "We need sanctuary." Then she remembered the way she was dressed. "I am no lad, but Lady Elena of Warwickshire." Then she gestured to Victoria. "This is the Duchess of Somerset. Please, we need your protection."

The priest tented his hands, as if in prayer. "God helps all in need. You are welcome here."

Relief washed over her. Would Nicolas honor the law of sanctuary? She doubted it, but hoped the need wouldn't be tested.

"Thank you, Father. We are blessed by your kindness," she gushed with a little bow.

The priest swept his arms out in a a grand gesture. "I'm Vicar Thomas. You both must be hungry."

Elena didn't need to look to Victoria to know she nodded, too.

He smiled kindly. "Then you are fortunate enough to have arrived when there's still food in our kitchen. Follow me."

Once in the kitchen, Elena and Victoria hovered in front

of the hearth while the priest prepared their food. The warmth from the fire felt devine.

"Please, make yourself comfortable," the vicar offered, pointing to the chairs near the fireplace.

Elena accepted a plate from the priest, tearing off a hunk of warm bread and stuffing it into her mouth. She scanned the room, stopping on Victoria, admiring her golden hair and blue eyes. Of course, they were same color as her son's.

Just then, Victoria looked up, catching her stare. "What is it?"

She shook her head, nervous to admit she'd been thinking about James.

"Do I remind you of someone?" Victoria asked, her eyes twinkling.

"Aye," she admitted.

"I understand more than you think."

Loud shouts coming from the direction of the sanctuary interrupted their conversation and the priest held his finger to his lips. But it was too late, a large sentry shouldered his way into the kitchen.

"They're in here," the man shouted.

At least five soldiers behind him shoved their way in.

Then, Nicolas emerged from behind the group. "What was lost is now found," he claimed in a superior tone.

Elena coughed. She stole a sideways glance toward Victoria.

"No one you need concern yourself with," the duchess answered, standing in front of Elena. Surely, he was surprised to find her with Victoria.

Nicholas stepped forward and rubbed his hands together. His rings flickered in the light. "Elena and Victoria under my command." His laughter echoed in the small space. "James won't have to choose after all."

Elena was devastated. All her efforts, lost. She wondered if the priest could help them.

"Sanctuary!" Elena cried out. "We claim sanctuary."

Nicholas let out chilling laugh. "Sanctuary? You're in the kitchen," he pointed out. "That only works in the church, my dear."

A sense of dread began to overtake her. Was it true? Could she be denied? She tossed a wary glance toward Vicar Thomas. His eyes were closed and he was praying.

Nicholas answered her question with action, ordering her hands bound as well as Victoria's. Another soldier hauled the priest off while she and James's mother were pushed outside.

Through the rain, a determined Nicholas directed their group to the bell tower on the other side of the grounds. Then, at the entrance to the belfry, a guard with an ax made quick kindling of the door.

Shoving her and Victoria through the entrance, cobwebs stuck to her face and hair. Cold air whipped in through the dilapidated walls.

Prodding them like sheep, Nicolas forced them to climb stair after stair until they reached the top of the tower.

When Elena was led close to the edge of the platform, her stomach roiled as she stared downward, into nothingness. God forbid if anyone fell from there.

"Now the punishment begins," Nicholas promised.

Grim faced, Victoria stared at Elena.

"You," Nicholas pointed at one of his men. "Tie the women up."

Elena was compliant as she and Victoria were secured to the wood beams above. There was nothing she could do to stop the guards.

"What happens now?" she asked.

Nicholas turned. "Isn't it obvious?" He rubbed his hands

together. "This is just the beginning. Once James finds you both dead, he'll come after me."

"You'll murder your own son?"

Nicholas glared at Victoria.

"Go ahead, Nicolas" the duchess said. "Tell us."

"Blood or not, I must eliminate any heirs that could challenge my claim."

Elena shivered, despising him more. When did he lose his heart? And if he killed James, no doubt he'd lose his soul forever.

"This is not Elena's quarrel," Victoria argued. "Let her go."

"I'm no fool, Victoria. The girl defied me. She must die for her disobedience."

"She was just being loyal to her knight," Victoria defended.

"More reason for her to die." He stood in front of Victoria. "You, the girl, James, and Richard. Die, in that order."

Victoria gasped. "Curse your black soul." She spit on his face.

He wiped his cheek clean with the back of his hand. "Hoist them up. I'm tired of this defiance."

The guard tugged on the ropes and Elena was lifted high, dangling over the edge of the platform. She shot a worried glance at Victoria. The poor woman looked so terrified.

Then the smell of burning wood filled her nostrils. Her gaze shot up. The rafters were on fire.

"God's speed," Nicolas called as he started down the stairs.

"Coward," Victoria screamed.

Nicolas's laughter filled the space as Elena choked on the smoke-filled air.

CHAPTER 23

As luck would have it, James was able to convince the gatehouse guard that he and Red were part of Nicholas's search party. After leaving the Garter knights in the hilltop woods outside of Cadbury Castle to keep watch for Nicholas's return, they rode hard on borrowed mounts, staying off the main trails until they reached the town of Sedgemoor. The Abbey was the most obvious place to stop first.

After they secured their horses, James walked toward the church and whistled for Dragon. The beast answered.

"He's here," James called to Red. "At least we know the women made it this far."

But once inside the abbey, they found it empty. Next, they made their way to the kitchen. Although it appeared someone had been there recently, his mother and Elena were gone.

Filled with disappointment, James led them outside again, hoping to find some evidence of the women's whereabouts.

Red knelt to examine the muddied ground at the barn's entrance. "I recognize Dragon's hoof prints, and our own, but here—" He touched the soft earth. "There are other tracks." He stood. "Perhaps they were taken back to Cadbury?"

That possibility sent panic through James. "Then we must return," he said, refusing to think he couldn't save them. "If it was Nicholas, I don't know how he got here first."

"A hidden path?" Red suggested.

"We must hunt them down," was James's answer.

* * *

NICHOLAS STOOD at the base of the bell tower and eyed his companion, Rudolph. "Victoria and Elena will soon be gone with no blood on my hands."

"No witnesses," his servant agreed. "Even the vicar won't be able to say what happened."

"I couldn't kill him." He breathed out heavily. "Even though I'm not a God-fearing man, certain fates shouldn't be toyed with."

Rudolf nodded. "The Vicar's death would have drawn suspicion. And you have much more killing to do."

He agreed. Nicolas had to destroy them all, James, Victoria, and the duke, to rule Somerset. It began long ago with the murder of his eldest brother. Then he became the sole heir to the Luttrell succession when he eliminated his middle brother before the king's coronation. "Soon I shall claim Somerset, Dunster, Nunnery, and Cadbury castles. It won't be long."

Rudolph laughed. "Holdings that vast might threaten the king's throne one day."

"Precisely," Nicolas agreed. Stranger things had happened in the history of England.

Then suddenly, he cried out—pain ripping through his

right arm. "I've been hit with an arrow." He confirmed it with his hand to his shoulder.

"Back inside the bell tower, Rudolf," he shouted. "We're under attack."

* * *

ELENA STARED AT THE FLAMES, wishing she could put them out with her thoughts. Curse Nicolas for tying them up in the tower. How would they escape?

Victoria coughed. "If he wanted us dead, that devil should have killed us."

"Don't give up," Elena pleaded. "Someone will find us. It's the Sabbath, and the villagers should be arriving soon for the service. The sun is rising."

"My throat hurts," Victoria complained, "but I can still scream."

Pop.

Elena shot a panicked glance above them. *Lord have mercy.* One of Victoria's bonds snapped, dropping her a couple feet.

They both screamed.

She didn't want Victoria to know she was afraid, but they were running out of time. If she was going to die, she needed to confess her deepest secrets.

"My lady, at Cadbury I told you the truth, but not all of it," she admitted. "I went to Warrick ready to damn James to hell, or demand he marry me. I didn't have the courage to do either. I know I can't live without him. And I don't know what to do."

"Sweet Elena, I won't judge you," Victoria said, coughing between breaths. "Only God can. But I can promise you this, if we're saved, I'll give James my blessing to marry you."

Elena's heart soared. Victoria's blessing was critical to any future with him. "Thank you," she said. Before she had a chance to say more, a commotion erupted on the steps below.

Nicholas emerged from the stairwell. "Who's getting married?"

As the earl neared, she noted his injured shoulder.

"Satan has returned," Victoria hissed. "Blood and smoke, we must be in hell."

"You're not dead yet?" Nicholas asked.

"Nay, but *you*, Sir Nicholas, will be very soon," a voice called from the shadows.

James? Elena held her breath.

Then her knight leapt onto the platform from the darkened stairwell wielding his longsword, fury darkening his face.

"Time is your enemy," Nicholas declared. "You can't kill me and save them at the same time."

James's eyes darted to the flames above. Then he rushed Sir Nicholas. "You killed my father."

"Impossible," Nicolas said. "I am your father."

"Lier!" James shouted with disgust and he shook his sword at Nicholas.

"Your mother will confirm it," Nicholas replied calmly, but took a step toward the stairwell as if he intended to run.

Will she? Elena looked her way, but the duchess hung lifeless from her bonds. *Fainted?*

James charged forward again. "You lie, cheat, and murder to serve your own purpose, why would I believe anything you say?"

"It's true," Elena cried out.

Swords locked. James shook his head, then metal clashed with metal again. It went on for so long. But finally Nicolas stepped away from James's reach, seemingly fatigued from the battling and his bleeding shoulder.

"Will you continue to fight me while your lover drops to

her death?" Nicholas asked, no doubt hoping to distract James.

"My lover?" James looked up, then lunged forward, slamming his sword against the earl's.

Should she tell him? She'd confessed to Victoria already. Yes, if she was going to die, he must know the truth. "I was the chambermaid at Berkley," she declared. "And your masked escort on Hocktide," she admitted. "And I…I love you!" Now that she'd confessed all, she realized he might hate her even more.

"I know," he ground out.

That's it? No sentiments?

Then he released his lock on Nicholas's sword and with a vicious cleave of his weapon, knocked it from the earl's grasp. It slid across the floor, going over the edge.

James turned from Nicholas and ran toward her. What was he after? Before she figured it out, he jumped over the gaping hole in the floor and grabbed on to the rope above her.

"What are you doing?" she gasped.

"Saving your life," he grumbled.

"How are you going to—" But she didn't get the chance to finish. The rope snapped. She screamed. And together, they went plunging into the darkness below.

CHAPTER 24

*H*ow had James managed? Elena would never know, nor could she get him to confess. Because she'd fainted, she had no memory of falling, nor of hitting the ground.

James had shrugged off all her questions and would only tell her that he had found a soft spot to land and Red had been at the ready to help bring both Elena and Victoria to safety. He was only angry because Nicholas had alluded them again.

As far as Elena was concerned, she was thrilled all three of them had escaped unscathed from his father's malicious plan as she waited for the celebration to begin that next evening.

Nunnery's great hall couldn't accommodate another guest. A grand reception to welcome Victoria home had brought all who loved her to celebrate. Elena sat at the high table, waiting like everyone else.

Finally, the duchess arrived on her husband's arm. And it wasn't just Elena who was in awe. Murmurs of admiration filtered through the room as James's mother made her way to the dais.

Of course she'd been with Victoria as they both'd been prisoners on the run, but the lack of nourishment and savage treatment, had taken its toll on the duchess until now.

Lady Victoria was dressed in finery fitting her station and she glowed with a confidence that could only come from the peace she carried inside her heart.

After the duchess was seated, her husband commanded the room with his wave of his hand as he addressed those gathered.

"Nicholas got away," the duke said, pounding his fist on the table. "I'll not rest until he's dead and buried."

"He'll meet the Devil soon enough if I have my way," James declared, standing up next to Sir Richard.

The duke placed his hand on James's shoulder for a brief moment, then straightened his tunic and gave his attention to the crowd again.

"When the duchess was kidnapped weeks ago, many of you stood beside me, suffering the same sense of loss I felt." He gazed at his wife sitting at the high table. "She's been safely returned, and now I can breathe again."

The crowd applauded.

Richard smiled at his wife. "We have Sir James and our Garter Knights to thank for her safe return."

Murmurs of congratulations swept the hall. Then the duke gestured to Elena sitting next to James.

"But let me not forget, Lady Elena had a hand in the rescue and she has been returned safely as well."

Lady Victoria then stood and gave her personal thanks to the Garter knights and she embarrassed Elena with what seemed to be an exaggerated tale of her actions in rescuing Victoria from the dungeons. It was a miracle the duchess had survived the abduction, imprisonment and Nicolas's final attempt at murdering her.

When the speeches were over, James turned to Elena at the high table. From his expression, she was certain he was still brooding over Nicholas's escape. She leaned over.

"You have my word, I'll not rest until he's dead."

He scowled. "I'm proud of what you've done to support my mother and I, but this is my fight, Elena."

She wanted to protest, but didn't. "I won't get in your way. I promise."

"That pleases me," he said. "But you are still under my protection. We must discuss this privately, in your chambers." He gazed at his mother. "I must have a word with Victoria first. I'll meet you shortly."

Elena left the hall and made her way to her chamber to wait for James. She didn't know what to expect from him. Her knight had every right to be angry with her. Would he accept her as his lover or send her back to her father as punishment? She paced endlessly in front of the grand four poster bed, unable to relax.

"Elena?" Someone called through the open door.

"I'm almost asleep," she called out, heading for her bed. She didn't want to see anyone but James.

With no warning, someone grabbed her from behind, covering her mouth so she couldn't scream.

"Of course you are tired," Nicolas said, "You nearly died."

Before she could move, he threatened her. "I'm holding a dagger to your breast."

Where is James?

"You left the church before the ceremony," he hissed, shoving a knotted piece of material into her mouth. "That was a bad choice."

* * *

VICTORIA WAS SURROUNDED by too many people to speak in private. James sighed and turned to go.

"Wait," Victoria said, grabbing his arm. "I've much to tell you." She kissed his cheek. "Let's find a place to talk."

They walked to a quiet corner.

"Mother, I'm troubled by my vows."

"I release you from your promise. It was selfish of me," she admitted. "I asked that of you because of my own failures. You have my permission to marry Elena. She loves you."

James frowned. Elena loved him? He wasn't certain about that. The girl's admission at the bell tower had surprised him, but it was the king who would have the last word.

"Not marriage vows, Mother. Sir Nicholas. I vowed to kill him, but—"

"Evil man," she said, interrupting him.

"God's truth," he agreed, but James needed to know the real *truth* about his father. "Am I his son?" he blurted out.

Judging by her pained expression, the answer wasn't what he wanted to hear. But he'd have to accept her response as gospel.

"Aye," she admitted with a sigh. "But there is so much to tell."

"I cannot believe you rutted with that man."

She gasped. "Please, James, you must understand. I've never lied to you."

"I only seek truth."

"I'd expect nothing less," she said, leaning against him. "Nicolas raped me."

"Raped you?" James roared, pulling away from her.

She winced. "I was carrying you shortly after," she explained, keeping her gaze steady with his, "but betrothed to Rafe and soon to be married. My father wanted to kill Nicholas," she confessed, "but because his family was powerful, he made a deal with him instead."

"A deal with the Devil," James muttered.

"My father banished Nicholas to one of our castles in Scotland. Because I was his only child, he agreed to give the Luttrell family Cadbury Castle after both he and my mother passed on, but only if Nicholas gave his word to stay in Scotland."

She paused. "Nicholas is the only son left in the Luttrell line."

James held up his hand. "This I know. I had a run in with him at Warrick Castle," he admitted.

"And his middle brother was to inherit Dunster Castle and become earl, but he was murdered just before King Henry took the throne," she explained breathlessly.

This was not new to him. That information had been confirmed as well. But he had another burning question that needed answering.

"A ring he wore—"

"A brilliant red stone, surrounded by a dragon's tail?"

James nodded.

"It belonged to Rafe. I hadn't seen it in years."

James was stunned. Nicolas must have taken the ring the night he'd killed Rafe. His face must have shown his outrage for she started to sob.

"I never told Nicholas you were his son. I don't know how long he's known." She covered her face with her hands again, sobbing more deeply.

He held his anger this time. The fact that he was not a de Saxton but a Luttrell was unsettling. Why did she hide the truth for so long? He reached for her trembling hands. "Why did you marry Nicholas then?"

"I know it's confusing. Nicholas coerced me into marriage after you left for the Garter, twisting truths to make me believe I'd lose my lands after my father died. When

I met Richard, he took care of everything, even the clergy. You two may not get along, but he's a good man.

"But it wasn't until that vile man appeared in my cell at Cadbury that I found out the bastard was still alive. Somehow, he knows who you are."

Standing, she gazed at him lovingly, tears streaming down her beautiful face. A lump stuck in his throat. He loved his mother and he hated to see her cry.

"Rafe was your *real* father, James." She hesitated as if she longed to say something else.

"Go on," he urged.

"I had a fight with Nicholas when he arrived at Cadbury the night Rafe was killed," she finally said. "I was the only one in the great hall with him. Nicholas demanded I turn over Cadbury Castle. My mother was still alive and I told him it was not his to take. Rafe heard our voices and came to my defense."

James was aching to say something, to tell her it was all right.

"I left them," she said, "and went to look for help. That's when you tried to fight Nicholas. But you were too late. We were all too late. It was a blessing from God that he didn't kill you."

"If he spared me then, why kill me now?"

Tears streamed down her cheeks. "Your father must have suspected you were a legal heir. You are in danger. Nicholas told me in the bell tower—you, then Richard—must die in that order. None of us are safe."

"Do not call him my father." James slammed his fist on the table. "Mother, please. The man will never be my father." He gave her hand a squeeze. "Now that I know, I must reinstate my promise to avenge Rafe's death and save our family from the earl's greed."

To his relief, a smiled graced her face before she said, "Do it."

Armed with his mother's blessing, he strode briskly down the hall to the women's solar. It was time to talk to Elena. Although, he'd still need the king's permission, now he could promise her a future together. Then, he'd hunt down Sir Nicholas to deliver his fate.

Once he arrived at her chambers, he found Elena's door ajar and drew his sword. Something didn't feel right. He pushed the door open with his boot. Empty? He searched and called her name, but Elena was gone.

Nicholas? He had to be at the root of this. He didn't doubt the man had traded his obsession for his mother, for his squire.

"God's blood," he swore to himself. Elena was in danger again and he had only himself to blame.

CHAPTER 25

"Marry us," Nicholas demanded.

"What in God's name?" The priest stepped back.

Elena's heart pounded as the earl forced her to stand next to him in front of Vicar Thomas. Terror gripped her. Nicholas was not a rational man.

"You heard me." Nicholas's men filled the small kitchen.

Yesterday he'd tried to kill her, now he wanted her hand in marriage? What was he really after?

"Is the woman here voluntarily?" the priest asked.

"She's here, isn't she?"

What could the vicar do? Nicholas would force her to speak the vows.

"Are you willing?" the holy man asked her directly.

She nodded. What else could she do?

"Marry us," the earl demanded again.

"Come with me to the sanctuary." Thomas reached for Elena's elbow.

"Nay, in here," Nicholas shouted.

"In the kitchen? A noblewoman is expected to marry in the sanctuary." He glanced at Elena.

"She'll do as I say." Nicolas offered the priest the Bible from the kitchen table. "I believe this belongs to you."

He accepted the book and thumbed through it. Elena was certain he'd try to help her if he could. But being surrounded by armed guards didn't offer any hope.

"God save you," the priest muttered, looking up.

"What is taking so long?" Nicolas bellowed.

"I've found the right passage, milord. Please, stand before me."

Nicolas once again grabbed Elena, tugging her into her position.

"From the book of Genesis," Thomas started. "A man shall leave his parents and cleave unto his wife . . ."

"No, just the vows."

With hands shaking, the priest fumbled through a few more pages, then started over.

"Nicholas, will you have this woman to be your wedded wife? To love and honor her, keep and guard her, in health and sickness, so long as you both shall live?"

"I will."

"Elena," he said. "Will you have this man to be your wedded husband? Will you love and obey him, in health and sickness, so long as you both shall live?"

Elena couldn't swear before God that she'd take Nicolas as her husband. Obey him? She'd spend her life defying him.

"I will finish this," Nicholas finally said. "We'll take her silence as affirmation." He growled. "Give me the Bible."

The priest obeyed.

With the book in hand, Nicholas stared at Elena. "I, Nicholas Luttrell, Earl of Dunster, take you, Elena, to be my wedded wife, as the Holy Church will ordain it." When he finished, he shoved the Bible into her hands. Then he drew his sword.

Hatred filled her heart. Even his manipulated vows spoke to his true nature. He loved only himself.

"Speak or I'll force the words out of your blasted mouth."

Elena slapped him.

Nicolas grabbed the front of her dress and shook her violently. "Repeat it," he demanded.

Marriage to a man she despised or death by his sword? She knew which offered the least amount of pain and suffering. But neither did she want to accept.

Her gaze darted around the small room, suddenly finding there was more than one exit. Attempting to escape was a risk, but she had nothing to lose.

She glanced at the priest, sorry he was caught in the misery. Then she gazed upward as she silently asked to be forgiven for her actions.

"Never will I obey you," she shouted at Nicholas as she tossed the Bible in the fireplace.

Vicar Thomas screamed, and rushed to a bucket of water nearby. Elena knew how valuable it was, but she had to do it.

Running to the door, she tried the latch, but it was locked. *Please God.* She backed up a few feet, then rushed forward, ramming it with her shoulder. "No," she yelled when it didn't open.

"Til death do us part," Nicholas mocked, stalking toward her. "Did you really think I'd let you go? Now you will die."

"Til *your* death do us part," a voice she recognized came booming into the small kitchen.

James. Elena collapsed against the wall. Relief washed over her. How did he know where to find her?

"You missed the wedding, dear Son."

James glowered, then stared at Vicar Thomas. The priest

nodded in affirmation. James eyebrows furrowed, but the news didn't keep him from confronting Nicolas.

"Never call me your son," he shouted. "You killed the man I considered my father."

Nicolas chuckled. "It makes no difference, you will meet your maker today. You are greatly outnumbered."

"No," Red countered, shoving his way through the small doorway. The rest of the Garter knights followed. "*You* are."

Elena gasped, overcome with emotion. Nicolas would pay dearly for his sins now.

"Let's finish this," James challenged, pulling his longsword from its sheath. "Red, remove the Countess of Dunster."

What did he call her? How dare he assume this mock wedding legal? By God, she'd set him straight. She sucked in a deep breath. "I'm as much that bastard's wife as you are his son. If you would have protected me the way any knight is expected to, I would have never been forced to speak those hideous vows."

James's eyes narrowed. His mouth opened, then closed, but he didn't say anything. Instead, he looked at the priest.

"In God's eyes, it may be binding."

James turned back to her. "I know how distressing this will be, but I must kill your *husband*, Elena."

"I would prefer to do it myself," she snapped.

James laughed. "We'll shed no blood in the Lord's house. Red, bind these men. We'll take them to Nunnery. I'll settle the matter there, on my terms."

As much as she'd prayed for Nicholas's death, the church was no place for revenge. She'd obey the only man she wanted as her husband.

CHAPTER 26

While Elena readied the armor in the pavilion, she counted her blessings. After all she'd been through in the few last days, she was happy to be alive and safely back behind the formidable walls of Nunnery Castle.

"Another joust?" Isabel asked, frowning. "Must honor and pride outweigh sensibility?"

Elena agreed and would pose the same question to James as soon as she found him. "Nicholas belongs in the tower, Isabel," she suggested. "Or better yet, in an unmarked grave. James insists on fighting him."

"Can't you talk him out of it?"

"Jousting is the Garter way. Besides, when has James ever taken my advice?"

Her cousin gave her a smug smile. "He listens to the stones."

Elena gasped. "You threw the stones for James?" She studied her cousin. "When?"

Isabel beamed. "You will listen to me now, won't you?"

She nodded, knowing full well that her cousin thought otherwise.

Isabel clicked her tongue. "If you'd listen to me when I threw the runes for you last, you wouldn't be married to Nicholas."

"That's not fair," she shouted, picking up a stray ax and waving it. "I'm having the marriage annulled. You know it was never consummated!"

Isabel ignored her outburst. "You weren't privy to James's company after dinner last night, but I was," she said, gloating.

"No, I was ordered to my bedchamber after the tables were cleared and put under guard for my protection," she complained.

Isabel helped fit the chain mail over Elena's head. "Are you sure about this?"

"We're talking about James's rune reading, not my attire," Elena snapped back, accepting Isabel's assistance with the next piece of armor.

"He questioned me about the vows he'd made to never marry. Asked if they could be reversed."

Elena held her breath, waiting for the rest. "What did the stones say?"

"Elena, I told James what I've told you. The runes don't tell you what *will* happen, but what *may* happen, when you open yourself to their wisdom."

"Yes, but did he speak my name?"

Her cousin shook her head. "I'm sorry, he didn't ask about you at all."

Elena bristled with anger, unsure what to think.

"You can't force him to marry you, Elena." Her cousin's tone was motherly. "But you can do everything in your power to make him want to."

His mother had already given her permission. Would the king? Or would James be required to leave the Garter, all he'd worked so hard for.

"Ready?" Isabel asked.

To risk disobeying James again to prove herself? Yes.

Yet, the armor weighed as heavily on her body as guilt did on her conscience. "If only James hadn't forbid me to fight, I could do as I please."

"One of the reasons I haven't rushed into marriage," her cousin admitted.

Elena flicked her a disgusted look. "Tell Fergus I'm ready."

Isabel nodded and squeezed her hand before she left.

Elena glanced down at her attire. She'd never worn jousting armor before. Never tested her skills so formally. If she could win, her training would be complete. She'd tell James, after she won the competition.

She sighed. Where was Fergus? She needed his help to finish dressing.

"Ready, my lady?"

"God's teeth," she shrieked, spinning around. "You startled me."

"Skittish as a horse." Fergus chucked. "Quickly now, there are only three ahead of you. But the draw as not been in your favor."

"Daylen?"

"Aye, my lady," he confirmed. "He's large, but clumsy."

"The squire or his horse?" Elena feigned a smile to hide her fear.

"The squire." Fergus chuckled as he finished with her armor. "Daylen charges at his opponents hoping that speed will give him an advantage. Don't play into his scheme."

"I will rely on instincts to direct my hands."

"God protect you, Elena." He proffered the helmet and she put it on.

Her resolve grew stronger as she walked to the stables with Fergus. Nothing would deter her, not even her love for James. She had her own reasons for fighting.

After the final preparations were complete, she crossed

the lower bailey on her horse, then found her way to the tilt-yard. A crowd had gathered in the stands. Even Victoria was expected.

Scanning the spectators, she found the duchess. But who was that next to her? Elena squinted. *Why is James here?*

Thankfully a trumpet sounded, drawing her attention away from him.

"Squires Fergus and Daylen, report," the official announced. Then the horn sounded again.

She was up next. A squire guided her mount to the tilt. The eye slits in her helmet limited her sight. But it didn't keep her from noting her opponent's great size. Fergus hadn't exaggerated.

"Lords and ladies," the herald called, "welcome Squires Daylen in green and Fergus in blue."

The crowd applauded.

Fergus. It was his reputation she must protect. Squaring her shoulders, Elena decided she'd better act like a champion if she expected to become one.

"One point for a touch, three points for a broken lance," the herald explained. "Five points for knocking your rival off his horse."

One hundred points if you are a woman capable of knocking your opponent on his arse.

"The squire with the most points after three passes will be the winner of the round."

Elena grew more restless listening to the herald explain the point system. Everyone in the crowd knew what a joust was comprised of. She sucked in a deep breath, ready to charge.

It was time. Elena pointed her lance directly at the heart of her challenger. Even though squire lances were hollow and lighter than typical weapons, she still struggled to hold it steady.

"Once I drop the flag," the herald stated, "the round begins."

Focused on the white flag, she waited.

The flag dropped. Her horse bolted into a full gallop, jerking her forward. When her arse dropped back into the saddle, she squeezed her thighs to hold on. She'd be the joke of the tiltyard if she was thrown from her horse.

Before she could blink, the sound of grinding wood against metal filled her ears. She rocked violently back in the saddle. But she smiled with pride when she realized her lance had shattered.

The crowd roared with approval.

"Three points for Squire Fergus, one point for Squire Daylen."

She returned to her side of the field, reaching for a fresh lance. Just as she got into position, the flag dropped again.

Daylen raced by her with no lance. She laughed, realizing he'd dropped it. Fergus had said he was clumsy. But she cursed herself for a missed opportunity.

Within seconds, she was at the end of the list and circling around the tilt ropes again.

"No points scored," the judge confirmed. "Squires, ready for the final pass."

The horses charged at full speed. She stiffened, tightening her grip on the lance as she braced for impact.

"Whack!" The direct hit knocked the breath out of her. She was falling.

"A perfect strike," shouted the official. "Five points for Squire Daylen."

Then everything went black.

CHAPTER 27

"Mother, why delay justice?"

Victoria shook her head. The crowd was cheering Squire Daylen's win.

"I can summon the bastard now and we can send him to hell where he belongs."

"Tomorrow is soon enough, my Son," Victoria said. "You won't rob your mother of her birthday wish, will you?" She gave him an affectionate pat on the cheek.

"Of course not," he said, "but after this event, the crowd would appreciate a duel to the death. A true contest."

She pointed toward the list. "It appears we may have one after all. Look."

James's gaze drifted. One of the squires was on the ground. "The lad's just stunned. No doubt it's his first joust."

"Nay," she insisted. "Red is waving to you. There must be something wrong. Go."

James hurried out of the stands. Red had pulled off the downed squire's helmet. Chestnut-shade, shoulder-length hair? Impossible. She wouldn't disobey him again.

By her side in moments, with Red and Tristan's help, they

carried Elena across the lower bailey and up to his solar. A tournament surgeon and Fergus joined them.

"Put her down gently," James insisted when they arrived in his room, "Make sure she is comfortable."

Then he glared at Fergus. "You." He pointed at the squire huddled in the corner. "Why did she take your place?"

"She insisted, my lord," the squire said, his hands shaking. "To prove herself for knighthood."

"Did she tell you I'd forbid it?" James asked.

"Nay." He turned red. "She told me she wanted to surprise you after her victory."

"And you agreed?" he demanded, stalking closer.

"I don't know what to say, Sir James. Forgive me."

"Get out," James yelled. Then he turned his attention to the physician. "Give me news. How is she?"

"Until she wakes, I cannot be sure. But she appears to be stable, breathing normally and no broken bones."

"How long until she opens her eyes?" His voice cracked.

"You'll need to keep vigil, check for fever, and keep her quiet."

"I will stay by her side," James assured him.

"I'll leave with the surgeon." Red patted his shoulder, staring worriedly at Elena. "Foolish girl."

"Wait," James insisted.

Reds patiently stayed until the door closed and he motioned for his friend to sit.

"You wish to discuss your plans to challenge Nicolas?"

"Not now," he said, checking Elena for fever. "It's not important right now."

"It is important," Red disagreed.

"Later. Did you know about her bloody plans to fight?"

Red scoffed. "No. if I had. I would've taken a switch to her arse and locked her up."

He nodded, unable to tear his gaze away from Elena.

"Why does she insist on acting like a man? Trying to become a knight?"

"She's a borne fighter."

James wanted to deny it, but he couldn't. He wanted to crush Nicolas's skull, make him pay for what he'd done to Elena, his father and mother, and now his life.

Red stood and squeezed James's shoulder.

He sighed. "Thank you for saying behind a while."

"Don't give up hope, James," Red said as he walked to the door. "I promised Isabel a report before Victoria's feast."

"Go. Tell everyone not to worry."

Finally alone with her, he clutched the cross at his neck. "Dear God, I promise if you bring Elli back to me, I'll make her my wife."

Imagining a life without her made his heart heavy. He couldn't live without her. Then it dawned on him. Everything Elena had been fighting for—training for, defying him for—had all been for him, not to prove herself worthy of knighthood. But worthy of his love. And she'd won. He loved her.

Duty and honor had blinded him. Not anymore. He cupped her cheek. "I love you, Elli," he said softly, kissing her lips. "Come back to me and I'll show you."

CHAPTER 28

"Happy Birthday, Mother," James announced proudly, then he gave her a generous peck on the cheek before taking the chair bedside her at the high table. "Elena sends her well wishes."

Victoria squeezed his hand. "I'm disappointed she couldn't join us, James."

Hopefully he'd been convincing when he'd answered her questions about Elena's absence. James wanted to keep the severity of her condition to himself. Knowing his mother, she'd demand to see her and cancel her party. It pleased him that Elena and his mother shared a special bond, but he worried they might conspire against him if they needed a majority.

"A toast." He raised his goblet. "To Victoria, may you always be loved by your husband, son, friends, and servants."

The guests applauded. The duke had spared no expense, and it made James happy to see his mother reunited with her husband and those who adored her.

Sometimes he wondered what it would be like to have such close relationships with people. He'd always been feared, even hated. But not loved like his mother. And now he'd wasted precious time pushing Elena away. Instead of welcoming her, he'd shown her his cold heart. Had he lost her forever?

Red entered the great hall and waved him over. James was anxious for news on Elena.

"Nicholas is secured," Red assured him as he reached for a serving of beef from a trencher.

"God's will, I trust."

"He'll be ready to meet the Devil whenever you decide it's time," Red promised.

"James—I—She—" Tristan was out of breath when he joined them. "She's awake," he told him. "Elena is calling for you."

Waisting not a moment, James raced from the great hall. When he reached his chambers, he burst through the door.

The healer turned. "Knock before you enter, can't you see she's very ill?"

James cursed, pushing the man aside. He knelt beside the bed, afraid to touch her.

"Is that you?" she asked in a breathless voice, her eyes still closed. She appeared too weak to lift her head.

"Stay still. I'm here, my love," he declared. Then he turned to address the healer. "You can leave."

"I'll be close if you need me."

James nodded, all his attention focused on Elena.

"James, are you there?" Her eyelashes fluttered. "Hold my hand."

She felt so cool to the touch, her tiny hand lost in his. If he could, he'd give her all the strength in his body. "I won't let go," he promised.

She sighed, her breaths shallow.

"Elena, I've been thinking . . ."

She let out a soft moan.

"I'm yours forever. Do you know that?"

"James—"

"Don't try to speak," he cut her off. "You followed me here to Somerset and have shown nothing but unfailing loyalty. More than any squire. More than any friend. Will you marry me, Elli?" He prayed her eyes to open so she could acknowledge his love.

"What of your mother's wishes?" she asked weakly. "Don't be pigheaded, you can't please everyone, James. You already made a promise to your mother and God."

He put a finger to her lips. Those lips he'd longed to taste again. "I already have my mother's permission," he reminded her. "Now I only need yours."

* * *

IT WAS all coming back to her. The joust. The fall. The pain. The darkness. But she was safe now. Warm. She'd heard James's voice. He was asking her a question.

"Elena, did you hear me? Do you understand?" James asked. "Just nod."

She began to move her head, but it hurt too much. "Whisper the answer." He leaned closer.

His words were garbled, but it sounded like he was asking permission for something. Was it the joust? She wouldn't approve of a new fight with Nicholas.

"No, James," she whispered hoarsely, "it's not right. You cannot put your needs above others."

Although she despised Nicholas for what he'd done to her and James's family, she was beginning to think it was wrong to wish him dead.

"I've my mother's permission."

"I don't care, you don't have mine." And then the world faded again.

Elena finished eating her buttered bread and hard boiled eggs. She'd saved the blueberry tart for last. Had she really been asleep for more than two days? Although her body ached, she felt ravenous. She ate the tart in two bites.

Someone knocked on the door.

"I'm awake." Elena scooted up on her pillows.

James entered, dressed in his knightly regalia. "Good to see you on the mend, Elena." His eyes swept over her. "The healer says you can ride tomorrow."

"A rematch with Daylen?" she joked.

James shook his head. "To return you Warwickshire." He turned to go.

Elena's head began to spin. "What of the joust? I must stay, at least to squire."

"I have honored your request, there will be no fight."

Her request? When? His icy stare stopped her from asking.

"Do you still seek knighthood?" He stepped closer to the bed.

Wasn't the answer obvious to him? "I've completed my training, proved myself worthy. All I'm lacking is the formal ceremony."

"Aye, that you have, Elena." He appeared proud of her. "No one will ever deny how worthy you are." He cradled her hand in his, flipped it over, then kissed her palm.

With James so close, her heart skipped a beat. She couldn't take another breath. "Why are you returning me to Warwickshire?"

"I'll take you home after we journey to Windsor Castle and St George's chapel, where the knights are dubbed by the king. We'll be at Berkshire for the festival. All knights must attend."

She wanted to believe him. "Are you promising I'll be knighted?"

"No, Elli, I can't. The law makes no exceptions where women are concerned. But we have a new king. Perhaps he'll consider a lady champion."

More than Elena had hoped for. She'd longed to talk with James about her future, their future. When they traveled as knight and squire, they'd spend hours together. Now everything felt too formal.

Without warning, James kissed her in a way that felt possessive. His lips claiming hers, with a forceful yearning, as if he'd been denied something he felt was his.

When he broke away, he said, "Isabel threw the runes."

She hadn't wanted the kiss to stop but she was curious about the reading. When she caught her breath, she asked, "What did the runes tell you?"

He tipped his head back. "To bed you." He began to kiss her again.

She moaned with pleasure, but planted her hands on his chest, trying to push him away. "I don't believe you."

"You know I've bedded you before?" He grinned.

"You pretended?"

"Elli, even drunk, I'm no idiot. I wanted you so badly at Hocktide, but not if it harmed your future."

Harmed her? If anyone found out about their few stolen moments of pleasure she'd be ruined. But she wanted more. If she couldn't have James as a husband, she'd be his lover. "James, make love to me."

The desire in his eyes was unmistakable. His smoldering stare cut through her. She knew what to expect.

"Are you sure, Elli?"

She wanted to prove that he was more to her than a means to knighthood and she kissed him savagely, bit his lip, rubbed her breasts against him, and tugged his hair. Were these not all answers?

But before she had a chance to shed her clothes and give herself fully to him, he caught her shoulders and pulled her away.

"Elena, I wasn't lying before, but the rune stones did not say when I would bed you." He tossed her a devilish grin. "I would love nothing more than make love to you now, but now is not the right time." He growled, stepping away from her, fisting his hands at his sides. "I must safeguard your reputation and your heart."

He turned and they gazed into each other's eyes. Love and fear gripped her heart. She was uncertain of what the future held. But at least she'd be leaving soon with the man she loved and nothing else mattered.

* * *

LATER THAT MORNING, Elena finished packing. Now that she was able to travel, she'd at least have another chance to be alone with James on their way to visit the king. Perhaps she'd get what she wanted after all. Her father and brothers would not hear of her indiscretions. A life with James was all she could think about, whether waiting for him at home or joining him in a quest. She met Isabel in the kitchen to say goodbye.

"Did James ask you?"

Instead of a hug or greeting this is what she wanted to say? "Ask me what?"

"To marry him?"

She rolled her eyes. "Nay. But I am content to be his lover."

"Remember, Elena." She shook a finger at her. "Men are ruled by their desires. Don't settle for anything until you're sure you know how he feels. The runes don't lie."

She understood, but wasn't interested in pursuing this conversation. "Good-bye, Isabel. I am off to St. Georges."

Isabel embraced her. "God's speed. And just so you know . . ." She leaned close to her ear. "Fergus and I are lovers."

"Fergus?" Elena smiled, understanding the need for a lover. She gave her cousin a huge hug. "Mind your own advice," she warned.

When Isabel stuck out her tongue and waved her hand in dismissal, Elena laughed to herself thinking back on how they both agreed to this sign up for this adventure.

After heading to the stables and mounting Winddogger, Elena summoned Myrddin, then joined Red and James at the portcullis gate.

James reached down from his horse to shake hands with Red. "I owe you a great debt."

"You saved me from a pirate's life, we're even."

James grinned. "Take extra care with Nicholas," he warned.

Red nodded. "Take extra care with Elena."

"What happens to him now?" she asked, wondering how they would keep a deviant like Nicholas under lock and key.

"Red has agreed to take the bastard to the tower in Mayfair." James frowned. "Victoria signed over all the Somerset lands to my name with the royal chancellor, including Dunster Castle. For now, Nicholas lives."

She nodded, satisfied with his answer.

"Safe travels, Elena," Red started. "But you are not traveling to St. George's on that old mare are you?"

"From your lips, to God's ears." She grinned.

A whinny sounded from behind them. "Am I on time?"

Elena spun in the saddle. Fergus led a beautiful destrier toward her.

"On time for what?" she asked.

"Elena, if you hold your tongue for a moment, you'll find out," James chastised.

She clamped her mouth shut.

"This handsome beast is for you, Elena," Fergus announced.

"Me?" She was already off the mare and staring at the warhorse.

"What will you name him?" Fergus asked, offering her the reigns.

She caressed the horse's neck. "Enchanter."

Fergus nodded with approval. "Walk him around the bailey before you ride. Get acquainted."

She spent the next hour doing so. And when James approached, asking if she was ready, she jumped into the saddle without his help.

James smiled. "More than ready."

And she was, desperate to see what her future held.

CHAPTER 30

On their second day of travel to St. Georges together, James found it increasingly difficult not to talk to Elena about her refusal of marriage. Even the weather seemed to match his mood, the increasingly threatening dark sky and violent winds battered the landscape. After he settled the horses in a lean-to, James walked inside the cabin where they'd stay the night and found Elena tending the hearth.

"Let me help you," he offered, pulling off his cloak and tossing it onto a chair by the door.

"I built the fire last night without any assistance," she said. With a little coaxing, the flames jumped.

Warming her hands by the fire, Elena appeared deep in thought. His gaze wandered slowly up her body. Everything about her excited him. How had he managed to control his feelings when all he could think about was her? He'd tasted her lips many times, now he craved the rest of her.

But Elena deserved to be courted, her heart won through sweet words and music. He walked to the chair by the door and retrieved his flute from his cloak. Let the music soften her mood. He played a few notes and she looked up, a small smile on her lips.

The longer he teased her with his song, the happier she became, tapping her toes and swaying her hips to the melody. God he loved to see her grin.

After playing a second tune, she clapped her hands and begged for another. This time, when he finished, he laid the instrument aside and edged closer, testing her willingness to have him nearby. He opened his arms and she rushed into his embrace, nuzzling against his chest.

"Elli, I really wanted to marry you," he said.

"We were children and you made promises any boy makes." She gazed up at him. "I cannot expect you to follow through with it now. It was a long time ago."

"Four days isn't a long time, Elena."

"What?"

"As you lay sick in bed, I asked you to be my wife again and you told me I was a selfish pig and rejected me. Don't you remember?"

"Nay. How could I possibly know what I was saying while I was delirious with fever?" She chuckled and gave him a courageous look. "Marry me!"

"Is that a question or a demand?"

"You decide." She laughed loudly.

He shook his head to make sure he hadn't imaged it. A sense of elation surged through him, but he didn't understand what just made her change her mind.

"Why now?"

"I never said no before. I misunderstood you." It was her turn to shake her head. "I thought you were asking permission to joust with Nicholas. I didn't want you to be in danger again."

He exhaled slowly, his heart pounding. He'd heard all he needed. The last thing he wanted was for her to talk herself out of it. Tugging her closer, his mouth claimed hers, stopping her words. His tongue slipped between her lips, dancing with hers. This is what he wanted. Feathering kisses down her neck, he cupped her breasts, loving how full and heavy they felt in his palms.

Then he scooped her up and carried her to the bed, laying her across the fur. Moonlight from the closest window streaked across her face, making her appear ethereal.

"Make love to me now, for we *will* be man and wife. Why wait?"

He sucked in a ragged breath and quickly shed his clothes. "Nothing will stop me then," he whispered, crawling on top of her.

Again he kissed her, his hungry hands enjoying the soft curves of her body. She wrapped her arms around him, moaning into his mouth as he deepened their kiss. But now, more than anything, he wanted to feel her silky skin against his.

He gently rolled off her, then started to untie the laces on her bodice. When he finished, her large breasts were completely exposed and perfect in every way he remembered. She groaned with pleasure as he suckled each nipple, his fingers tickling her arms at the same time. He hiked her skirt up with one hand, then repositioned himself on top of her, fitting his shaft between her legs.

Her eyes widened in delight as she bucked against him. Sweet, sweet Elena. He circled his hips, enjoying the sweetness he felt between her legs.

"Are you ready, dear Elena?"

She gazed up at him, her sly smile the answer he wanted.

As he threaded his fingers through her hair, their lips met again, and he thrust gently, piercing her core.

"My love," he whispered, kissing her neck. "You are the

greatest prize, my greatest accomplishment." He thrust again and she cried out.

He stroked her cheek. "It won't hurt again, I promise."

"I trust you," she answered with conviction, then she wrapped her legs around his center, hugging him tight.

James responded, pumping his hips fully sheathed.

It had taken this journey with her to prove his life was laking, even though it was full of accomplishments. He never should have denied his feelings after he'd uncovered her secret. Curse his bad judgment and denial. He loved her. Nothing would change that.

And if he didn't pace himself just right, he'd lose control on the next stroke.

Reaching between her legs, he caressed her while he moved inside her.

She let out a tiny sigh, matching him stroke for stroke.

Moments later, their bodies slick with sweat, Elena cried out in fulfillments.

He followed, screaming her name and clinging on to her as if he'd never let go.

CHAPTER 31

*E*lena glanced about the unfamiliar surroundings of the abandoned cottage. The fire had gone out. The only light came from the moonlit window. Still wrapped in James's arms, she was warm, tucked up tightly against his stomach. He wanted to marry her? At least that was what she remembered.

He stirred and she rolled over to face him. "Last night I dreamt that *I* asked *you* to marry me," she confessed.

James opened his eyes, studying her face. "Nothing you have done or said since we've together been together has been customary, my love." He brushed a stray hair from her face. "Did I say, yes?" He laughed.

She stared at him, his eyes dark with desire. She wanted him again.

"I love you, Elli. I should've said that long before now, but I was too proud. A knight's way of life doesn't allow for much love and comfort. I'd all but shut it out, until you forced your way in." He brushed the back of his hand tenderly across her cheek. "I will be yours forever."

"I love you too, James," she pledged. "Though I must

confess it hasn't been a secret, it still feels new to say it." She hugged him tightly, giving him a deep kiss. How could she be this lucky? Everything she'd ever dreamed of rested in her arms.

She wondered how Isabel would react to the news that she was going to marry James. Of course she'd say she'd predicted it.

James propped his head on his arm. "Elena, I want nothing more than to make a day of this, but we must be up and on our way to St. Georges before the sun rises." He gave her a peck on the forehead, then crawled off the bed. "The knighting ceremony is only a few days away and we need to leave as soon as possible. I'll ready the horses."

She sighed when he left. All the warmth escaped with him. She packed their few belongings while she waited. A few moments later, the door opened.

"That was quick," she said without turning around. "You're almost as fast as your squire."

"Almost."

She cringed at the sound of Nicolas's voice. Dread gripped her. How had he escaped? Maybe there was some truth in James calling him the Devil.

Nicholas bellowed with laughter. "Is that any way to greet your husband?"

She kept her back to him, willing her heart to stop beating so erratically. She wheeled around. "What do you want?"

"You," he said, taking measured steps toward her. His soulless eyes stayed focused on her. But the ruby ring on his finger drew Elena's attention as it always did. Only this time, he didn't cover it up.

"You knew I'd be back for you."

No, she didn't. He was supposed to be on his way to the tower. He'd signed a treaty, made amends. The last thing she expected was for him to follow her here. Where was James? She gazed about the room searching for a weapon. James's longsword waited near the hearth.

Nicholas must have guessed what she wanted to do, because he lunged at her, blocking her path to the sword. He grabbed her, flipped her around, and held her against his body, taking a blade to her throat. She resisted the urge to fight and let him push her outside.

Relieved she didn't see James dead on the ground, she kept silent, hoping and praying her knight was close. To her surprise and dismay, there were no horses in sight. Not even one for Nicholas to ride away on. What was his plan?

A whirling sound came close to her ear. She screamed when Nicholas collapsed behind her and the dagger clanked onto the wooden porch.

Gasping, she stepped back, glancing down. Nicholas was bleeding from his left temple, a stone near his head.

"James?" she called.

Nothing moved in the moonlight.

Too afraid to stand outside waiting for him, she remembered James's sword and hurried inside. Just as she grasped the weapon with both hands, Nicholas staggered through the door.

"Woman, I don't know how you did it, but you'll not strike me again," he vowed. "I'll be done with you before you have another chance."

"I did not—"

"You must be a witch," he accused.

"She is not a witch."

James. How many times had he come to her rescue? Thank God he was alive. She didn't even have time to think before James grabbed the longsword from her hands and sliced through Nicolas's chest.

The earl hit the floor.

She held her breath.

James towered over Nicolas. Kicking his side, the earl didn't respond.

"Is he dead?"

James finally nodded and met her gaze. "He cheated death so many times. I was not about to let it happened again." He gave her an overall assessment. "Are you hurt?"

"No," she whispered, still in shock. Everything had happened so quickly.

James nodded and opened his arms.

Elena didn't hesitate and ran into them. She began kissing him all over his face. "I thought you were dead." Tears stung her eyes.

"We were lucky that Nicholas was so arrogant that he assumed we were traveling alone." He hugged her tightly. "That's why I didn't call out to you on the porch. I needed to make sure all in his small muster were killed by our contingent of Garter knights." He pulled back to gaze at her. His expression grave. "I didn't see Nicholas until it was almost too late, my dear Elena."

She prayed no one dear to James had been hurt. "I wonder if he killed anyone at Nunnery when he escaped," she said.

"We'll find out soon enough." James let her go, then knelt beside the body. "I want my father's ring."

She eyed him. *Father?*

"Rafe's ring," he clarified. Then he yanked it off Nicolas's finger. "'Tis not good to talk of the dead, but my last words are God's will is done."

Elena stared heavenward, thankful they both had survived one last battle with the former Earl of Dunster.

CHAPTER 32

James didn't regret killing Nicolas. He'd saved Elena, and nothing else mattered.

Arriving with her at Windsor Castle that morning, he was quickly reminded of his first visit to St. George's Chapel for his own knighting ceremony. Favored for its fortress defense, Windsor was now the main residence of the new king.

After Elena was settled in the tower, James made his way to the king's private chambers, optimistic that his royal highness would honor his requests. Fortunately, James had fought alongside Henry at the Battle of Bosworth. He hoped the monarch would remember his loyalty.

"Your Majesty," James said, leaning over Henry's hand. He kissed his ring.

"Rise, Sir James." The king dismissed his servants.

"Sire, I will be brief," he said, taking a seat at the counsel table. "Your cousin, Nicholas Luttrell, is dead." When the king didn't react, he continued. "I killed him."

"You did me a favor."

"Excuse me, Your Majesty?"

"He threatened peace and would soon challenge my throne."

James's mood lifted. If he'd done another service for his country, perhaps the king would grant his wishes.

"Sire, with your permission, I would like to make a personal plea."

Henry nodded.

"Sire, I brought the daughter of your armorer, Sir Guy, to court today. Lady Elena of Warwickshire."

"Go on."

"There's no simpler way to say this. She deserves to be knighted."

The king regarded him. "That's a highly unusual request."

"As one of your champions and Garter knights, I ask you to give this serious consideration. This lady has fought with more courage than most men. She saved my life and abides by the chivalric code. I've taught her all I know. She's Garter-worthy."

"A Lady of the Garter?" the royal muttered.

James clung to hope.

"A new house, demands new rules. I'm prepared to make bold changes. James, if you say she's worthy, than she's earned my esteem as well."

The king started to get up.

James shifted in his seat, but didn't rise with Henry. "Sire, I've one more appeal."

The king sat back, then steepled his fingers.

"Would you honor me by making the lady knight, my wife?"

"To leave the Garter?"

"I do not take my oaths lightly. But I will give up everything to marry her."

"Will it change your allegiance to me?"

"No, Sire," he answered honestly. "I'll be more God-fearing because the lady will expect it."

The king laughed. "Rise and stand before me," the king commanded.

James obeyed.

"Does the woman give her consent?"

"I wish to surprise her."

The king chuckled and stood to leave. "Then you have my permission and my condolences if this does not go your way."

James breathed a sigh of relief and took a bow. He could only hope when she became Lady of the Garter, Elena would still found him worthy.

* * *

"Shh," don't disturb her, my lady." The servant stood with Elena outside the chamber door. "She's meditating. I think that's what she calls it." The young girl covered her mouth to suppress a laugh.

Elena recognized a familiar scent, musk and jasmine. "Enter," a voice called from within. "I can keep your secrets, *Señorita,* but can you guard the ones I give you?"

Elena walked into the room. It looked much like the pavilion tent at Warrick Castle.

"Come, *buena Señorita,* come in, do not be shy. Take a seat."

Is she hiding again?

Elena scanned the room, then stepped over the pillows on the floor. Memories came flooding back from her first meeting with the seer. Elena knelt on the cushion closest to her.

"Looks can be deceiving. One may appear as a woman one day, a boy the next."

Vertina stepped out from behind a painted screen. "Will you be his wife?" The gypsy smiled at her.

"I followed James on the journey. I was tested in ways I can't explain." She wanted to say more, but Vertina probably knew what she was thinking.

"Your visit here is no coincidence. The spirits have called you back."

"It's the king, you see." Elena was flustered.

"Of course I see. I see *your* future. But do not ever forget, you have the power to change it."

Elena considered what the woman said. She'd told her that before. Fiercely loyal to the runes, Isabel and Vertina both swore by their power, but also claimed power came from within. How could both be true?

Letting go of all her fear and doubt, she smiled at the gypsy.

"One rune," Vertina said, "that's all you need."

Elena reached into the red velvet bag, thankful her hand didn't shake like before. She wasn't the same girl. She'd dressed like a man, fought like a man, and slept with a man.

Last time, she'd asked about her future with James. Didn't she already have the answer?

Vertina looked puzzled when Elena didn't withdraw a stone.

She shrugged her shoulders. "At first I thought I needed to see the future to find out who I was, but I now know I must trust my heart."

The seer smiled. "A guide's work is done when the seeker finds their own truth." She stood. Then before Elena had a chance to thank her, the woman vanished.

Elena shivered. Had a spirit just brushed her shoulder? It was time to face her fate.

It was only a few hours later, trembling with anticipation, when she walked into St. George's cathedral, the honorary chapel for the Garter knights, ready to test her fate. James had promised he'd take her appeal to the new king. She hadn't seen him since this morning and wasn't sure he'd even gained an audience with his royal highness. She took a seat in a front pew.

Eventually, the Garter Knights quietly filed into the sanctuary, forming a semi-circle before the altar. James winked at her as he passed, dissolving some of her doubt. When the king entered and took his place behind the pulpit, it was time for the ceremony to begin.

After the Lord's Prayer, the king raised his arms. "I'm honored you've joined us today in celebration of our patron, St. George. Here in this cathedral, your banners are displayed, the vigil to honor your deeds are promised, and your dead are kept."

After more prayers and readings, the king performed the dubbing ceremony for two knights. Just when Elena thought the ceremony was coming to a close, Henry gestured her to join him.

"It is my honor to bring forth another deserving squire to join the Most Noble Order of the Garter, Lady Elena of Warwickshire."

Murmurs of approval drifted through the pews. But both panic and excitement struck her. What she'd longed for was finally coming true.

She knelt before him and Henry raised his hands over her head, reciting in Latin.

After he rested his sword on her right shoulder, she swore to protect the realm and king. After the short ceremony he sheathed his ornate sword.

"Rise, Lady Elena," the king commanded, then gestured for James to join them.

Once he was at her side, she stared at her knight, wondering what would come next. *Isn't the ceremony complete?*

"Marry us," he said to their monarch in a strong voice, then smiled down at her.

"Is the woman willing?" the king asked.

She nodded, feeling lightheaded.

James wrapped an arm around her waist. "I won't let you fall." Deep emotions flickered across her knight's face. This was real. Her dreams were coming true.

Then a man with a slight limp, started down the aisle toward them.

Father? Is this man my father? She was shocked. Once he reached them, he smiled. With a wink, he placed her hand in James's.

"Now, Elena," the king said. "Repeat everything you hear."

She did, not missing a word, careful to protect what she'd fought so hard to get. Finally he said the words she'd been waiting for.

"You may kiss your knight."

James gazed at her and with a wink, leaned down and stole what breath she had left with an endearing kiss. A kiss to seal their fate.

After the king blessed them, the cathedral erupted in applause. As they began to walk down the aisle as man and wife, Elena saw something that made her stop. When she realized who had joined them, she shrieked with joy. God must have forgiven her sins, because everyone she loved was seated in the sanctuary, her brothers, Red, Victoria, and Isabel. She stared at James.

"Good news travels fast," he said.

Isabel was the first to congratulate her on the steps outside. "I threw the runes, they told me to come. I invited everyone else."

Elena couldn't help but laugh.

"Remember," Isabel added, "you did this all on your own."

"I know."

Her cousin grinned. "Of course you do. As much as the runes guide us, if we believe in ourselves, we can shape our future."

Just then, Red and Victoria joined them. Her brothers and father crowded close, too. When the king stopped to congratulate her, Elena bowed.

"I am ready to be of service to my king," she offered.

Her brother William stepped forward and bowed beside her. "Sire, she is an excellent food taster."

She frowned, glancing around the circle of loved ones. Her eyes narrowed on William.

"Would you excuse me, sire," she asked. "I need to show William some of my new fighting skills. It was he who encouraged me to become a knight. Do I have your permission to defend your castle, even if it means killing him in the process?"

"As you wish, Lady Champion," the king agreed. James handed her his sword.

Although it was quite unladylike, she hiked up her skirt and started down the steps after him.

"Get back here and fight like a man," she yelled.

"Elena, don't hurt me."

James's laughter warmed her heart. Some things would never change, and Elena was all right with that.

Also from **Crown & Castle Publishing** and **Marisa Dillon**:

THE GOLDEN ROSE OF SCOTLAND (The Ladies of Lore Book 2)

When poisonings are an everyday occurrence, healer Rosalyn Macpherson must be ready with an antidote. Unless it's for the English Lord who means to claim her clan's Highland castle.

What's in a name? Everything, for Lord Lachlan de Leverton, a charismatic English aristocrat. He'll break the law to sever his ties to his notorious family. But first, he must secure the deed to Fyvie Castle before the feisty Scottish lass wins it.

Because of their conflicting claims, Rosalyn and Lachlan are ordered to appear in Edinburgh's royal court, and in an unusual twist of fate, they are assigned as guardians, rather than prisoners, to a caravan carrying the Golden Rose, a papal gift for the King of Scots.

When the royal decree becomes a forced marriage between the two, it's not the remedy Rosalyn had hoped for, but now she doesn't hate this Englishman as much.

Before the knot is tied, the Rose is stolen and Lachlan's suspected of the crime. Rosalyn then faces the hardest decision yet. Must she sacrifice her precious Philosophers Stone or the land she loves, or both, to save him?

Available on Amazon: **THE GOLDEN ROSE OF SCOTLAND**

THE SECRET OF SKYE ISLE (The Ladies of Lore Book 3)

A lifesaving antidote grows as a rare rose on an isle full of faerie lore. Healer Ursula Fraser won't risk delivering her best friend's twins without it, but first she'll need a guide and a miracle.

Both come in the form of battle-scarred laird Alasdair MacLeod, a Highlander who seeks to avenge his father's death and claim the title, Lord of the Isles. He requires an heir, not a wife. But when he offers her his guidance, he also offers her his bed and a bargain.

Insulted, but fearless, Ursula expects she'll convince the laird to do her bidding without sacrificing her morals. Her ability to conjure herbal potions gives her great power until she discovers the Scottish laird is the only one who can save her from the murderous MacDonalds.

Will this Highlander who harbors a family secret keep her from returning to Fyvie Castle in time for the twins' delivery? Or will a faerie prophecy filled with magic and a roll of the dice settle all the scores?

The answers lie in *The Secret of Skye Isle*.

Available on Amazon: **THE SECRET OF SKYE ISLE**

THE DUCHESS HEIST (The Art of Love Series 1)

What is the cost of a nude painting from the Royal Academy of Art?

That depends on who you ask.

Possible ruination . . . for Lady Lillias St. Clair, the daughter of a gambling-addicted duke, when she discovers a partially completed portrait of herself reveals her identity and much more. But before she concocts a scheme to steal it from the prestigious academy, the artwork goes missing.

Perhaps salvation . . . for Lord William Cavendish, who hides his dark past behind a cavalier air and his good deeds. Yet, to earn true redemption and raise funds in time for a grand gesture, he must enter an international art contest with a scandalous pose of an unknown figure model, who turns out to be the daughter of the duke who stands between William and his dreams.

Worth dueling over? Both families have fought a generations-long feud between them. So when a fake engagement presents a chance to recover the missing nude portrait, Lillias and William agree the ruse may prevent a scandal.

When reputations are at stake, and a nude painting hangs in the balance, the cost could be too high for either of them until they find what Shakespeare once wrote to be true: 'love's not time's fool.'

Available on Amazon: **THE DUCHESS HEIST**

ABOUT THE AUTHOR

Connect with the Author:

With a bachelor's degree in journalism, Marisa has spent many years writing for the television industry. As an award-winning producer/director/marketer, she has worked on commercial production, show creation, product branding and social media.

Marisa has always enjoyed reading romance novels and now fulfills a dream by writing romantic adventures not for the faint of heart. *The Duchess Heist* is her first book in the Art of Love series.

Visit Marisa at: www.marisadillon.com.

Goodreads:https://www.goodreads.com/author/show/10792736.Marisa_Dillon

BookBub:https://www.bookbub.com/profile/marisa-dillon

www.ingramcontent.com/pod-product-compliance
Lightning Source LLC
Chambersburg PA
CBHW060322310726
48976CB00007B/2408